A FOURTH FACE

Also by Grant Tracey

CHEAP AMUSEMENTS

TORONTO, 1965: CHEAP AMUSEMENTS' BEAT

FINAL STANZAS

LOVERS & STRANGERS

PARALLEL LINES AND THE HOCKEY UNIVERSE

PLAYING MAC: A NOVELLA IN TWO ACTS,
AND OTHER STORIES

A Fourth Face

Grant Tracey

A Hayden Fuller Mystery

Twelve Winters Press

Published by Twelve Winters Press, a literary publisher.

P. O. Box 414 • Sherman, Illinois 62684-0414 • twelvewinters.com

A Fourth Face was first published by Twelve Winters Press in 2018. It is also available in hardcover and digital editions. The character Hayden Fuller and the phrases "A Hayden Fuller Mystery" and "Hayden Fuller Mysteries" are the property of Grant Tracey. All rights reserved.

Cover and interior page design by TWP Design.

Cover art copyright © 2017 Miles Wisniewski. Used by permission. All rights reserved.

Author photos copyright © 2018 Mitchell D. Strauss.

ISBN
978-0-9987057-5-0

Printed in the United States of America

for Ted

A FOURTH FACE

The past is never dead. It's not even the past.

— WILLIAM FAULKNER

1

"They think I did it."

His voice was buried shells on a beach, thin creases, full of sand. I didn't recognize it at first.

I squeezed my eyes in an effort to open them more fully. They were caked with cereal crust and the shadowy figure before me was a series of rocks floating by the side of my bed. I propped myself up on my elbows.

Thin traces of moon lit his shoulders and the tips of his chin and hawk nose.

"Bobby?"

He opened his mouth without speaking. The clock on the nightstand glowed 3:40 or 8:17. It had to be 3:40—it was too dark to be morning. My face was hot but my forehead was cool and the ceiling fan twisted with a slight rattle.

Anyway, I hadn't been sleeping well. My therapist says I got shit to work out. That's how she talks, "shit to work out." The 1960s is a progressive time.

I have this reoccurring dream: I'm trapped in a musty suitcase, full of moths, my father's bourbon-soaked voice yelling, "get out, get out." I'm never sure, in the dream, if he's imploring me to fight and free myself from the suitcase or to extricate myself from his life. Get out.

"I saw her. A plastic bag." Bobby dropped his forehead into his shoulder, his voice taking on more sand. "I didn't do it—"

The rattle of the ceiling fan was louder than I expected it to be. It was as if some of the sand had slipped inside its bearings.

Bobby Ehle was an ex-Leaf defense man, and tonight his face was full of little scratches like he had fallen down an ivy trellis or some such damn thing. There were deeper marks around his Adam's apple and along the tops of his hands. His hockey story: at the start of the 1964 season, after being a seven-year pro, three-time Stanley Cup champ, and second-team all-star the prior season, he retires, leaving training camp in Peterborough, Ontario, having had it with my ex-coach Hugh "Two-Fisted" Farrell, a regular resident philosopher. "Hockey's a game of emotion, Ehle, it's a streetcar named desire, and I don't think you've ever caught it."

Two Fists sure loved that line. He said it to Big Z, me, Billy Harris. He should get a patent on it or one of them registered trademark things. You know with the R and the circle? Anyway.

I think Gordie Howe has one next to his name. Really.

You can look it up.

I'm kidding. Who the hell would do such a thing? He's known as Mr. Hockey, but he's not full of himself, and Bobby was known as the Pest, the Intimidator, and the ever so pithy moniker Little Shit. The latter was only uttered behind opposing teams' locker room doors, a shared space that the press had limited access to.

I guess Bobby eventually caught a different streetcar than the one coach was riding. I don't know what he'd been doing the last year or so. One time, I saw him in back of the Gardens, near Church Street, smoking a cigarette, signing autographs. It looked like the last place he wanted to be, but there he was, shoulders hunched, chin on chest.

As I adjusted to the shadow light, the marks on Bobby's hands became more apparent. The skin around the fingernails was nicked up, gouged, and flecked with dried blood.

And his voice. It wasn't the same. The fast rat-a-tat-tat he had as a player was now full of beach sand and much slower than I remembered.

The real reason Bobby walked away from hockey? He was depressed. His wife Nancy had cheated on him with a plastic surgeon, Cliff Airedale, a tall angular guy with a baggy ass and a hitch in his walk, a guy who should carry a tennis racket wherever he goes, a guy who thinks a goatee makes him Beat Generation–cool.

I took the pictures of their "interludes" with a Leica and fast film so I know how baggy his ass is.

Bobby had hired me. It was my first "case." Before snapping covert pix of Nancy and Cliff I took mainly photos of the fellas' girlfriends and wives, sexy snapshots to keep in a cedar chest or the far recesses of a desk drawer. The Bobby case helped pay for my new Hi-Fi. Unfortunately, the dividends didn't outweigh the full cost. The story of the affair broke when my girlfriend at the time, Stana Younger, reported it in the pages of the *Toronto Telegram*, and I wound up drummed out of the NHL for "moral turpitude." Bobby played the rest of that season without me, and then hung up the skates after a few weeks of training camp, summer 1964.

It was now a year later. Summer, 1965. July. Nancy Ehle had returned to being Nancy Drouin. And I had the feeling Bobby wanted to hire me again. Something about the sand in his voice.

"Plastic bag?"

"Yeah. It was on her face." He grinned a troubled corkscrew leer, like he couldn't get things to add up in his head. He always had that look as a player, in practices, during games, while playing cards on long train rides. It was a look inhabiting a vacant parking lot and at the same time an intense stare filled up with crammed cars, stories he couldn't share. Now the voice was heavily medicated.

"She's dead?"

He nodded. Slowly.

"And you—saw her?"

"I was following her." He looked away. A scar, the chunk of a golf divot, was a small river creasing his lower lip, and the skin around his eyes were puffy leeches, the face of a boxer. Bobby was tough but he was dirty. He led our team in penalty minutes every year, scrapping with the likes of a Lou Fortunado, and one night at Madison Square Garden, Lou-doo tried to tomahawk Bobby's hair from his scalp with sharp clutching hands and razor-like forearms, and Bobby knocked him cold with an overhand haymaker, but he didn't take off his gloves. You don't fight with your gloves. Hockey code. But Fortunado had treated Bobby's hair as if it were an unwarranted accessory, and Bobby just lost it. Did he do the same thing with Nancy? Did he hit her with gloves on?

"You had a restraining order." I reminded him of what I read in the dailies, Stana Younger's column. Every goddamn day. "You're supposed to be nowhere near her—" He had been previously arrested, including sixty days ago, but Nancy dropped the charges.

She did that on more than one occasion.

"I know, I know." He shrugged, his left ankle turned awkwardly. "I wanted another chance—" He rubbed at deeper scratches on his left cheek. There were sharp, parallel lines, three tines on a fork. He scrubbed his tan-colored hair, trying to remember something.

"She's not your wife anymore—"

"I know, I know. I got the memo, okay?" His chocolate-brown eyes filled with remnants of a corkscrew leer. "To be honest with you, I don't know how I got to her apartment. I was just there." He leaned his forehead into a flat hand and steadied himself. "And I saw her—"

There were lots of things he couldn't remember anymore. Too many concussions. "Who was number 15. On the Leafs," he asked. "Fifteen?"

For some reason it was important to know this, now.

"Billy Harris," I said. Our fourth-line center.

"Four?"

"Red Kelly." Our best backchecker, next to Keon. Shut down Béliveau.

"Seventeen?"

"Me." I smiled, my face hurting a little. "Hayden Fuller." Drummed out of the league for a "hobby."

"Right, right." He remembered his "D" partner, Bobby Baun, and our goalie Johnny Bower, and the Captain, Benjamin Small-bear, but their faces, and highlights from various games, like the overtime winner he scored in '61, were all disappearing, shallow puddles lifting up from a hot sidewalk.

I don't know if it were because I only had two hours of sleep, but suddenly the whole room was full of sand, in my eyes, behind my eyes, in my mouth, in my head, on my skin. It swirled about like a dust storm. It stuck everywhere. I felt like I was in Oklahoma, 1934.

"What's with the scratches?"

He shrugged. "Barroom scuffle? Habs fan?" The joke wasn't getting any play. Maybe the timing was off. He delivered the line two beats too slow.

"Look at your hands. The scratches around your neck. Some-one was fighting back. Desperately." One of the fingernails on his left hand was torn off.

I was now circling him. "Why were you following her?" My knees hurt a little.

"I wasn't *following* her."

"You just said you were."

"I mis-spoke. I was just. There. Like. There."

"What suddenly you're Tinkerbell now, floating through keyholes, magically appearing in people's apartments? C'mon Bobby, level with me."

"I don't remember."

"Did you kill her?"

"No." He shrugged.

The ceiling fan needed an adjustment or two.

"I was worried about her, I guess, so I wanted to see. Her."

"Worried. What do you mean?"

"Airedale's bunch. She's mixed up with them."

Well, she had been sleeping with him, the guy in need of a tennis racket.

That ended a while ago. They were still friends, Bobby said. Imagine that guy being. Your. Friend? "I've seen them at his clinic. Guys with gloves on their hands."

"Gangsters?"

What was Bobby doing at the Queen Street clinic?

He couldn't remember the name of the clinic. Neither could I.

"Hitmen," he said, nodding. Slowly. "That's the kind of guys who wear gloves." He raised his shoulders. "Did you hear about that publishing house in Montreal, the one that publishes literary novels that nobody reads?"

Literary. When did he learn that word? In his playing days all Bobby ever read were comic books and racing forms. He really liked Hawkman. Said they had similar beaks.

"Yeah." I read the story. A fire burned down half the building, delaying the release of several titles, including a new collection of poems by Leonard Cohen.

"Nancy overhead Airedale's crowd vaguely. Talking about. It. Taking sideways credit."

"Uh-huh."

"Nothing specific."

"Right."

"And then there was that English paper in Montreal—"

"*The Citizen*?"

"Yeah."

A small bomb was found in the lobby with a threatening note attached, something about those who tell the stories having the power. The bomb squad rushed in and uncovered three or four faux wires, discovering it was nothing but a smoke bomb, a variation on a mild teargas canister.

"Same outfit?"

"Maybe."

My stomach was full of cold rocks but everything else about me was gritted with sweat and sand. I needed a shower.

"Believe me, Hayden. I never hit her. Ever." He reached into his shirt pocket and dry swallowed some pills. A lot of pills.

And those hands. A fingernail missing.

"That's not what the papers said." I was still circling. "The scratches? Those are fresh—" The lower part of my back was on fire. I leaned left, right, stretching. Maybe I needed a new bed.

Stana last week ran a three-part feature, an exclusive story with Nancy Drouin, detailing Bobby's depressed moods as a player, his melancholic outbursts, his intense jealousies whenever Nancy talked to another man. He'd punch her again and again and yelled, "Don't you ever disrespect me. You hear what I said. Don't you ever—"

"We'd scuffle a little. In the past. That's all."

"What about tonight?"

"A little." He pushed a hand against his forehead. "I think. I'm not. Sure. God, I think. My head hurts—"

"You remember 'scuffling'?"

"I think so."

"Your head? That's what the pills are for?"

"Yeah." *Like I was telling you, Hayden, concussions.* He'd had a lot of fights in the pros, and sat out a dozen or so games each season with excruciating pain, black dogs barking about in his head. One time, the pain was so bad, that before a game Bobby was lying on the locker-room floor, his head resting against the cool concrete.

Coach stepped over him as he rattled on about desire.

The ceiling fan whirred like a helicopter. I was still circling.

"C'mon Bobby—the truth—"

"I was just there. And the plastic. Bag."

"You were just there? Scuffling." I wondered if he'd take a lie detector.

"Hell, yeah. Lie detector. Fuck. Yeah. Wrestling. That's all. Scuffling. I never, ever, punched her. I pushed her sometimes when she got a little crazy, slapped her back when she slapped me, but I never punched her. You got to believe me." The whirring got louder.

I looked up at the ceiling fan. "What the fuck's with that?" I wasn't very good at fixing things. Toasters, lamps, light switches, forget about it. My pop never passed on basic electrical skills, or carpentry or masonry, nothing. I was good at making phone calls.

It wasn't the goddamn fan, he said. "Helicopter." *That really cracked him up. You think a fan can get that noisy, Hayden? He was still laughing, crumpling over. Maybe it was helping with his headaches.*

"In my backyard? A fucking helicopter?"

He was heading to Oslo, Sweden. Oslo's in Norway, I told him, and he said he always sucked at geography, but the place in Sweden sounds like Oslo, it has an "O" in it anyway, a lot of O's, but for now the helicopter was taking him somewhere up north, bush country, and from there he was going to make his way to Sweden to coach hockey. "They want us Canadians over there. They say Terrien's there too."

Brian Spinner Terrien was buried in a plot of land about to become an amusement park. But only I and a handful of people knew that. Stana knew.

"Sweden. They have extradition, Bobby—"

"This will all blow over by then."

He'd be in *Oslo, Sweden* in less than twenty-four hours.

"I'm hiring you to find out who killed her. The real killer." He shook his head again. "A plastic bag, man." He popped another pill, and the laughter stopped, a match puffed out.

Was she seeing anybody?

No. He nodded. "Well, maybe Terry."

"Who's Terry?"

"Some fucko she met at the clinic. Terry Quinton."

I wrote it down on a yellow pad by my nightstand, next to the clock, and my .38, in its holster, loaded.

Bobby's shoulders suddenly shook. Nancy's death eyes, man, were shiny coins. Bright and much bigger than they should have been. He absently touched one of the tines on his cheek.

"I don't know if I can take these headaches much longer. Sometimes I figure—"

I handed him a glass of water.

"I loved her."

I bit my lower lip.

Blades whirred.

My mind drifted to the suitcase and my father, yelling.

Shit, I don't know how the helicopter even landed in my backyard without waking the whole fucking neighborhood. I live in the suburbs, a kind of Toronto Levittown, where every fourth house is the same. Fortunately, some of the houses around me haven't been finished yet. The house to my left needed sheet rock added to the upstairs frames, and the two houses to my right were on bald brown dirt, awaiting the additions of mats of grass. But my yard was a different story. A helicopter sat like a huge black dragonfly filling up space, kicking up puffs of dust. I hadn't mowed in weeks. It looked like South Vietnam out there.

I could make out some markings on the copter, KEY. It was black and white and the front windows tinted. Who was the pilot? Bobby couldn't even drive a car, well not well. He was the worst, taking his hands off the wheel, frequently, to make whatever point he was bloviating about. He was no Richard Petty. "Who's flying the bird?"

"Was I really a second-team all-star my final year?"

"Yeah."

He nodded, his lips pushed together, and he looked away, his voice dropping. "A friend. Flying the insect." He handed me five hundred dollars. Slowly. They were crumpled and resembled fat worms. "That's all I've got." His face was boyish, bashful, as if he were afraid of being in trouble. "Don't be mad at me."

"I'm not mad. Who's flying the bird?"

"You look mad."

"I'm just trying to figure things out."

"That's just for starters. The money? What do you call it?"

"A retainer?" It was more than generous. My fee was $40 a day and expenses.

"Yeah, that. Retainer. Will you look into this?" He crushed a hiccup in a big shoulder. "Help me?"

"I got to tell you, Bobby. It doesn't look so good. The evidence, I mean?"

I'll take a lie detector. In Sweden. Send it to you. He wanted so much for me to believe in him. He was like a little kid. "You're really not mad at me, right?"

"No, Bobby."

"You sound mad."

"Jesus Christ. I said I wasn't. I'm not. The bird?"

He reached for his pills. They were tiny bird bones in his big hands. "I didn't do it." He dry swallowed.

Maybe it was the headaches. I get them too. Maybe that's why I decided to help him. "How will I get in touch?"

"You won't. I will." He took down my number. Here and at my office near Yonge and Bloor.

"Okay." Look, I told him, I had to play this cautiously. Not make a big ruckus. I was trying to get back into the NHL. The Montreal Canadiens had invited me to their summer tryout camp; GM Sam Pollock had even visited my house and we talked about art; he too was a big fan of the Original Seven and A. J. Casson, but NHL President Clarence Campbell didn't care much for Pollock or Montreal or Casson for that matter (the Philistine) and blocked my ability to play anywhere in the NHL next season. However, Soupy said if I continued to keep my nose clean he'd reevaluate my chances for reinstatement later this summer.

"The Habs?"

"Yeah."

Bobby shook his head. Slowly. "I'd love to have played. For the Habs." He was from Laval, a Montreal suburb.

My getting banned from the league wasn't quite on the level of the 1955 Rocket Richard case or any reason to riot, but the Montreal fans sure were kicking up a great big noisy fuss saying the NHL was once again pitting itself against the French Canadian team and everything French Canadian. I guess I had become a bit of a celeb for solving the Stabulas, missing girl case. Got good press notices. Even Stana wrote me up a two-page spread in the *Tely*.

Got some good business out of it too: a woman whose cat, yes Felix, had gone missing, and a fella who thought his wife was cheating on him. She was. With another woman.

Bobby had read the *Telegram* spread. That's why he was here. He liked how I operated.

I reminded him that I didn't even know how to fix light switches.

"Bilingualism in Canada has always been about being French and having to learn English," Bobby reminded me. "It's never the other way around." He shrugged. "You speak French?"

"Un petit peu."

"Je me Souviens? That's the name of the outfit that Nancy knew about and runs with Airedale's crowd. Was. Running. Or Airedale was. Taking credit for? Shit, I'm not sure. Je me—no. That's not quite the name. Something like that."

I remember. Bobby couldn't remember much of anything.

The floor creaked as Bobby ambled to a dresser and looked

at himself in the mirror. He wiped his tired eyes and didn't like what he saw. And then he traced his face in the glass with his fingers, or hand, at least that's what it looked like from where I stood in the angular lights of moon. He was writing words on his face, trying to erase his face with words, but there were no words on the mirror. Nothing.

Just his face: vulnerable, sad. That's something, my therapist argues that I struggle with, being more present in my feelings. I was supposed to be taking a rest cure. On my last case, I had killed a man, a miserable fuck who raped young girls and exploited women, and everyone felt like *I needed time alone, to heal.* My therapist said I wasn't dealing honestly with my emotions, my past, my relationship with my father (why is it always about the father?), and I needed to truly listen to that voice of discontent that tells us all is not good, but I wasn't hearing any such voice, not even late at night when I couldn't sleep. "Vulnerability is the key," she said, *let go of things and admit what hurts.*

Maybe I needed a new therapist.

And what was there to admit anyway?

I guess I should tell her about my reoccurring dream, the one with the damn suitcase. She's into Jung and dreams.

"Yeah, I read about that too," Bobby said. Slowly. "You blew him away. Head shot. He got got. Got what he deserved. Abusing women. That guy was a real lowlife."

I don't know if he saw the possible connection to himself.

Irony is not a strong point with hockey players.

For Jane Austen, whom Stana adores, yes. But hockey players, not so much.

Bobby was definitely bigger than I remembered, his pants hitched under his round, hard belly, his belt a notch too tight. Certain meds can slow you down and pack on the pounds, I guess.

"The scratches, Bobby? From Nancy? Before you killed her?"

"Look, Hayden. You're my friend. Would I ask a friend for

this kind of favor, if I wasn't speaking the truth?"

"You would if you were desperate."

He moved from the mirror, his face disappearing into the shadows of moonlight. "I *am* desperate, damn it. After Stana's articles, who's going to believe that I didn't do it?" He hitched up his pants and returned to the mirror. Maybe he saw other faces there that I couldn't see.

"Hey, she's just doing her job," I said.

"I'm sorry. You're. Right. I forgot you two had a thing."

Not anymore, not after her tie-ins with Babe Migano. But the two-page spread in the Tely *was nice.*

"Look into Airedale, the doc, he's running some kind of racket and I think he killed her."

"What kind of racket?"

"Maybe that publishing house. I don't. Know. Nancy hinted at some things—Cassel for chrissakes." He shrugged, looked at his fingers, and smiled his perpetual corkscrew leer.

"Drugs?"

And then he mumbled something about blue pills.

"What kind of pills?"

The ones he was popping were white. I noticed. Tiny bird bones.

"Damn." He screamed, his voice a short burst from a .45. His head wasn't working right, goddamn it. He couldn't remember the name. But blue was the color of the pills, and at least some of his migraines were blue. Like. The. Pills.

"You said something about Cassel, Lenny Cassel, Detroit kingpin? Did Nancy tell Stana about Cassel and his possible involvement with Airdeale?" *It was probably her next big story, knowing Stana. I'd have to see her again and get the skinny to follow the thread.*

Maybe I'll return the photos. I have a couple of nude art photos, okay five or six, I took of her back in '62, when I was learning my craft, and we had a thing going. I still look at them, occasionally.

"Yeah. Damn straight. Lenny Cassel. Detroit mobster."

He was a sick, scary fuck. A slight man, thin in the shoulders, but the eyes, burning snakes. Lenny had disappeared three-four weeks ago after a witness testified to the feds that she had seen him kill a prominent politician and reporter in a black, shaded alley. He used a machete. Chopped the shit out of them and tossed chunks of limbs into green trash bags. Lenny thought he was alone but a restaurant owner, tossing a different kind of refuse into the trash, saw the murders. Lenny has been hiding since. Reports had him spotted in three American cities and two in Canada. Nancy saw Lenny at Airedale's clinic.

"You're sure?" Maybe he was involved on some kind of drug front. The blue pills.

"Maybe. Nancy. Told. Me. She saw him."

I nodded.

"I used to go to Cliff's clinic. He does some kind of hydrotherapy. Water treatments and electric shock."

"And blue pills."

"Yeah. The pills helped. For. A. While." They calmed him down, relaxed his headaches.

"I thought Airedale was a plastic surgeon?"

"He's a doctor, ain't he? Has his hands in a lot of, let's say, projects." Airedale's clinic specialized in out-patient procedures, the removal of moles etc., and also electric shock and hydrotherapy for depression. He's got a ton of famous clients, including actors, that guy on that TV western with the spotted dog—and the sidekick who wears a top hat? Always says cheerio?"

"Uh-huh." Bonanza–lite that show. "I thought you hated Cliff."

"I do." But Nancy had gone there. "You know he worked on her nose? Yeah. Took the bump out of it—"

"I see—"

"And that's when I saw all those men with gloves on. Something's going on there and Cassel's involved."

"Could Cassel have placed a plastic bag over a woman's head?"

After all, he had hacked two people to death with a machete. What could he do for an encore?

"Anything's possible with that cat." He smiled his corkscrew leer. "Nancy talked to Stana. Told her things. See the reporter."

Stana. I wasn't looking forward to the idea of seeing her. Maybe I should wear new shoes.

The blades whirred louder.

Stana. My stomach still had this empty space in it, like a hole, over what had happened before, my last case.

Stana. In a way I did want to see, if, as my therapist suggests I was really being honest with myself, and my complicated feelings toward Stana, new shoes or old shoes.

Bobby waved goodbye and before I knew it, the slow walking Ehle was under snapping blades, the yellow moon a slice of lemon.

He never did give me the name of the damn pilot.

And then the nose of the dragonfly came back towards the earth, up, down, and lumbered, over fences, houses, and I wondered if it would ever stay above the horizon line.

On to Oslo; Sweden that is.

Jesus Christ, that just cracked me up.

2

The pictures weren't pretty. Eight-by-ten's. Black and white. The focus off, a little messy. Police crime photographers weren't high-end shutterbugs, but there was enough sick evidence here to hammer home the point: Nancy Drouin was beaten repeatedly, horribly. Exhibit A: dark half-moons under her eyes, a split lip, and a hard hockey puck rising up out of one of her cheeks; Exhibit B: two chipped teeth and an open cut from a ring's sharp edge along her chin; Exhibit C: hair shorn away from above her left ear, like a patch of torn carpet knashed by an angry Rottweiler. These weren't autopsy pictures. These were post-domestic abuse exhibits, beatings courtesy of one ex-husband, Bobby Ehle.

"How can you be working for this fuck?" *Stana.* Her voice a fallen icicle.

How indeed.

It wasn't some moral code. I believed my client, in the emotions behind the words. Sure the evidence wasn't stacked in his favor, but in my line of work talking to people is more than just reading words, it's about reading psychology, and my instincts were telling me to have some reasonable doubts.

Stana huffed, shuffled the photos, her eyes sharp freckles, the lines on her hands raised. She was wearing a long brown skirt, a dark blouse, and a cardigan with diamond-shaped buttons. A small scarf traced about her neck like a feminine bow tie. A pencil was behind an ear. The fragile lines of her face were almost translucent, bare china against such fine bone structure.

She tapped the tip of her chin.

Top Cop Sal Lambertino was nodding along with Stana's tip-tapping. He apologized for being unable to get us access to the crime scene photos, yet, but, man, once I saw those I'd be "puking through my eye balls. They're disgusting. I've never seen such a beating." He leaned up against Stana's desk and played with the fringed off fence ends of his Hemingway beard.

Stana's desk was cluttered with loose paper, memo pads, pens in a glass, flowers in another glass, and seven or eight ceramic coffee cups. One of the cups was red, green and brown and had an Aztec vibe.

Sal let out a short breath, raised an eyebrow, and wondered if I was a dumbass or what. *How could I be helping such a person?*

"Sal, I've already heard that melody, huh?"

"Well, you're going to hear a lot more, pal."

He was also pissed at me for not reporting Bobby's visit—the absurd helicopter rendezvous—at my house a lot sooner. "What were you thinking, Hayden?"

"Apparently I wasn't," I said.

I thought I was being ironic. They read it more as an abject apology. I guess in a way it was.

I wanted to tell them both about the dream of me and the damn suitcase.

Sal must have got promoted after our last missing girl case, Cathy Stabulas. He was now a plainclothes guy: gray flannel suit, white shirt, gray tie, gray fedora, a regular Sloan Wilson.

"I like the new look, Sal. Very Joe Friday."

"I'm not in the mood for jokes."

"Just the facts, huh?"

"You're pushing it—"

"Sorry."

"From what you told me about Bobby's hands, the missing fingernail, the spots of blood, those are clear indicators of someone who probably just killed somebody else." He shrugged absently. Lit a Rothman's. "Or super-tuned them really fuckin' bad." He blew smoke in a far corner of the room.

One of the overhead fluorescent tubes needed to be replaced. It was blinking dimly.

I couldn't disagree with their feelings.

But somehow my instincts were telling me that the killing was much more complicated than it appeared, that Bobby, despite his record of domestic abuse, may not have been fully accountable for what happened. Those damn blue pills. His memory loss. How did that figure? Hell, he couldn't even remember Bobby Pulford, one of the greatest two-way Leafs ever.

After my client left, I couldn't get back to sleep. So I wandered the dark lonely streets of Toronto, my heart punching my chest and shoulders, as rain fell in gentle perforated streaks. I ate a donut or two. That didn't calm me down. So I ate a third donut. And a fourth. Cream-filled. And then I came here. To Stana.

And now I needed her help. Again.

I didn't bring the photos. The ones I took in '62. I thought about it. Really.

"We're looking into that helicopter pilot. Nothing so far." Sal shrugged. There was loose thread in the suit's weave, the crease where the shoulder meets the sleeve. "Jesus Christ, who lands a helicopter in a backyard?" He laughed. I wanted to tear away the thread.

"I know, right?" I laughed too. My face hurt a little. I had eaten two donuts too many.

I had needed Stana's help on my last case. Three months ago. I wondered if she were still on Babe Migano's payroll.

"If I didn't like you so much, Hayden. I'd run you in—for sitting on that as long as you did." Sal jabbed a finger into my chest. It hurt. I think it was intentional.

I gave him my lopsided, lupine grin. My head was full of

dirty cotton candy, a world slightly thrown off axis. Shit, I wish I had some of Bobby's white pills.

A water cooler gurgled and typewriters clacked and paper scratching across platens filled the silences between our words. The fluorescent tube still blinked dimly. I pushed back the brim of my porkpie. "Where were you taking the story next, Stana?"

"I didn't have a next." Her fingers curled along the rim of an adjacent coffee cup. It was the "Aztec" one, the one I had bought for her in Mexico in 1963.

Men, in the open-doored office behind us, spoke in rushed voices. The Leafs had just traded Danny Davis for Marcel Pronovost. In the offseason, Davis had complained that Hugh "Two Fisted" Farrell had overworked the boys in daily scrimmages and they were "too tired" to beat Montreal in last year's semi-finals. The Leafs lost in six.

"That's too bad, huh?" I pointed to the adjacent office door. My face had a sneer to it. I hated Davis.

Stana looked away from their office and rubbed the edge of a wrist. She was no longer interested in the sports pages. She too, like Sal, had been promoted, writing hard-hitting features, focusing on the lives of women. Two weeks ago the emphasis was on unequal pay in the work force. This was the week before the Nancy Drouin abuse story.

"The paper wouldn't let me run the photos." She shrugged and reached for a cigarette. Parliaments. An English cigarette. Her favorite beer was Guinness. Irish. Something seemed at odds there. *Like her personality, full of quirky contradictions. Could I trust her, again? Could I?* "The publisher said no photos. Surprise, surprise, huh? Another fucking cover-up, mustn't explore truths that would shine a negative light on the wonderful sport of hockey."

Stana tossed the photos in front of her. The stack fell apart and crumbled across her desk blotter. She flipped hair behind the ear without the pencil.

I don't know when she started smoking.

"What did you expect?" There was no challenge in my voice. Shit, Stana worked for the *Toronto Telegram*. It was a conservative paper, with ties to Imperialism and England. The *Tely* always endorsed the Conservative Party. Every goddamn election. Is it so surprising that they wouldn't want to print such photos? Too salacious, the higher-ups would say. Such photos challenged patriarchy, the very system the *Telegram*'s editorial staff and publishers reinforced. "Maybe you ought to work for the *Star*?"

She shot me a sulky look. The *Star* wouldn't offer her enough money.

"I'll get you the autopsy photos, Stana, once I get the green light from upstairs." Sal's eyes were lean. "Nice guy this Bobby Ehle."

It wasn't like I wanted to stare at the photos before me, but it was hard not to. Nancy's eyes looked blackened, forever wandering in the dark, like me this morning, lost, walking heavy in the light rain. It was as if whatever optimism she had once believed in could no longer be summoned up.

I feel like that a lot.

Stana sighed heavily as she exhaled. "Nancy wouldn't press charges." She shook her head in disbelief. It was an ongoing pattern, women blame themselves, she said. "How fucked up is that?"

"Pretty fucked up." Lambertino shoved his hands deep in his pockets. He'd seen it over and over again as a cop. The worse call to respond to was a domestic disturbance. Any cop will tell you that. "Shit, I got a knife in the shoulder one time—from a wife. I had been subduing her husband who was whacking her with a hockey stick." He rubbed at the phantom wound. The loose thread of his sleeve was gone.

Scuffling, Bobby said. These photos didn't back that story. This wasn't scuffling, wrestling, or slapping her down when she slapped him. This was full-fledged fisticuffs and maybe yesterday he went too far, maybe he just might have killed her. But his voice, the tears. They were so sincere. I wonder how he'd do with a lie detector test?

And the plastic bag? That little rhetorical flourish wasn't Bobby. No way.

"When we found her body, hours ago. She had been beaten to death. And then the plastic bag was placed on her head." Sal's fists tightened inside the pockets of his trousers, pushing against the fabric like an outcropping of moon rocks.

"You mean the bag was—"

"Post-mortem. Some kind of special effect. A calling card. I don't know." *She was already dead, Hayden.* Sick fuck.

I wasn't sure if he was referring to me or Bobby.

"Any chance it could be Lenny Cassel?" *He had a way with machetes and trash bags. Did he add plastic bags over faces to his repertoire?* "I hear he's in town. Nancy saw him—"

"She never told me that." Stana's eyes were full of freckles.

"Bobby said—"

"And you believe what Bobby said?"

"I'm with Stana." Sal leaned further into the desk's edge.

I'm surprised his thighs didn't have splinters.

"I wouldn't trust anything a man who beats up women has to say." He shook his head. "Besides, does he remember anything accurately? From what you told me, the guy's brain's fried." He took a short drag.

Fried. I wasn't crazy about Sal's choice of words, but Bobby sure couldn't think like he used to. And he couldn't remember much either.

"Look, Hayden, you yourself said the scratch lines on his face were fresh. He didn't get those in a bar fight."

"No."

"And the torn fingernail—"

"Right."

"So how did he get like that?"

Bobby never did directly answer that.

What if I got him to take a lie detector test and he passed? Would it help muddy things a little? Would it point the arrows of this case in different directions?

It might, Sal said, but he didn't think Bobby could pass a polygraph here or in Oslo, Sweden. I had told Sal that joke twenty minutes ago and he, no doubt, thought it was worth repeating. Bobby would be overseas in a few hours. "Under Nancy's fingernails we found traces of skin, blood, and hair. We'll get a match. Trust me."

"What about Airedale? What's his racket? Curing depression with hydrotherapy. Electric shock. Bobby looked like he was fucked-up on meds to me."

"How so?"

Typewriter keys rat-a-tat-tatted like coins slapped on counter tops.

"Everything he said was really slow. Like he had to think before he could walk or nod his goddamn head." And the words full of sand. The voice, *the whole room*, full of sand. I felt like I was walking in his sand, right now, that I couldn't get up hill. "And he kept muttering something about blue pills."

"That's interesting—"

"Why?"

Stana took another drag. "Yeah, why?"

Sal placed his hands on Stana's desk, and leaned across, both eyebrows raised. I could smell his Old Spice aftershave. The police *had been* looking into Airedale's clinic; there were rumors from two different informants of mind-altering experiments involving LSD Blue 27, a special hallucinogen that takes away pain, but slows people down. You no longer have any inhibitions but you no longer have any desire either. The competitive edge is gone. The drug hasn't been licensed, but the Canadian Army had been experimenting with it to help returning vets combat battle fatigue and maybe Airedale got a hold of some. He had served as a medic in Korea, 1952. "Right now these are just rumors, so don't print this shit. Stana, you read me?"

She smiled. It was good to see. "Right." She doffed an imaginary cap his way.

I was glad she had kept the coffee cup I had got her in Mexico.

The early '60s was when the drug was first introduced, Sal said, a French-Canadian scientist invented it. Sal couldn't remember the name. He took off his hat and scratched his sandy-haired head.

"Hey." I looked at my watch. "It's my birthday." July 17th.

I just said it without thinking. I do that sometimes.

Sal smiled. "Congrats." He laughed. "We were working the day watch out of Bunco. The captain is Stana Younger, my partner is the Birthday Boy. My name's Lambertino."

That just cracked me up. His Webb-like intonation was impeccable.

"Don't ask me to do that again. I mean like ever." He straightened the cuff of his left sleeve. "My birthday gift to you."

"Thanks."

Stana nodded, her imaginary cap now doffed in my direction. The lone fluorescent tube still blinked dimly, announcing its separation for the bright track lines of the rest.

"So you think Nancy knew about this, the blue pills, and they killed her?"

"*He*, Bobby Ehle, killed her," Stana corrected me. Her jaw was tense and her hands looked like sharp flags.

"It's a possibility. I'm not ruling it out. The blue pills *is* the wild card," Sal confirmed.

"Could Bobby and Nancy be partnered in something, something illegal, something—maybe involving LSD blue 27?"

"Nancy and Bobby? Fuck no." Stana took another sharp drag and crushed what was left of her cigarette in a shallow ashtray.

It was a sign that my allotted time with her was running low on minutes. Subtle.

"Oh, and another thing about your alleged client." Sal stabbed an even stiffer, stubby finger into my chest. And it hurt more than the last one. "Remember when I said if you saw the autopsy photos you'd be puking through your eyeballs?"

"Yeah. The whole puking through my eyeballs thing? Not an expression I'd care to re-visit, Sal."

"Whoever slugged Nancy, used heavy fists, breaking the orbital bones around her eyes and arranging her nose so it no longer would fit her or any face. It was as if the assailant wanted to lift her whole head off her shoulders with his fists. A guillotine with his hands." He shook his head. "You like Picasso?"

"Not particularly," I said.

"A goddamn Picasso painting," he said. "That's what she looked like. Abstract art."

Sal's not one for hyperbole.

Unless he's pretending to be Jack Webb.

How could someone on the calming effects of LSD Blue 27 do such a thing?

"He'd done all these other beatings." Stana's hand hovered over the brick of photographs crowding her desk. "It's a pattern—"

"Yeah, but he was slow last night. His reaction time. If he was on LSD Blue 27—"

"Maybe he took the hallucinogens after killing her, to numb the pain—" Sal said.

Typewriters clacked. A water cooler in the far corner of the bullpen still gurgled. *But the pills he took after were white. I saw them. Little bones of birds.*

"So what do you want?" Stana blew smoke from a freshly lit cigarette into a near corner of the room. "Why are you here, Hayden?"

"Help. That's what I want. Look, I'm just doing my job, Stana."

"He did it, Hayden. *Look* at these pictures. That's his third face." She stared me down, her blue eyes darkening with anger, and then threw a photo at me and said Bobby's third face was on full display. Photos don't lie. "That's a man who can kill and did."

She sat back in her chair, hands behind her head, arms two triangles, a tense pulse line running along her jaw. "Maybe what he said sounded so real to you, so sincere, but—" She piled the photos, corners lining up. "You ever think, Hayden, there might be a fourth face?"

"Huh?"

"The three faces *you* told me about. There's the one we have in private, the one we have in public, and the one we don't even know we ever had, the one that emerges and shocks us under extreme conditions like combat or insane psychical obsessions. And this friend of yours is obsessed."

"That doesn't make him a killer."

"You hockey players sure stick together—"

"That's not fair."

"Blood brothers for life? Is that it?" The water cooler was no longer gurgling. "A fourth face denies what the third face ever did and convinces faces one and two and the world that the third face was a part of someone else, another time that doesn't matter. A fourth face is a face of denial, a fourth face counteracts the third face, proving the lie that you can run from yourself, hide from who you really are." She pressed her hands deeper behind her neck. "Bobby truly believes he didn't do it, even though he knows he truly did because that Bobby is not the *real* Bobby." Her thin smile stretched into a sad line. "You killed a man, Hayden, and feel no guilt about it whatsoever. You told me as much."

"I did." My upper lip trembled slightly.

"What's that but your fourth face denying what your third face did?"

Jesus Christ. "Maybe." I shrugged. "You might have something there."

"I think you should fire your therapist and hire her, birthday boy." Sal shadowboxed my shoulder and chin with soft air punches.

"You see a therapist?" Stana lowered her eyes.

"Yeah." I shrugged. "Of course."

My confession got her to smile slightly.

I like it when she smiles, her whole face and eyes take you in. *Damn, I thought I never could feel for her again, and now some of it was coming back. Damn.*

Yes I needed her help but I also wanted it, wanted to need it, wanted her.

"Any idea on who was flying the helicopter?" She tapped the pencil against her lower lip.

"No." I smiled, my lopsided grin. I told them about the letters KEY on the side. That's all I could make out. There was just too much sand. "You have any ideas?"

"I'm not going to be your partner—"

"You want to get Nancy's killer, don't you?"

"You let him get away," she said.

I smiled.

And maybe, just maybe she was right.

3

I bowled a few games to clear my head: 120, 163, 155. I throw a straight ball. Never could figure out how to put a hook in the damn thing. Get more action with a hook. Anyway, after three games, I grabbed a hotdog, with mustard, yellow peppers, and kosher pickles, from a street vendor, ate on the run and belched my way up the stairs to my office.

I love Hebrew Nationals but they always do that to me.

Thank god I passed on the onions and a side order of roasted chestnuts.

Outside my frosted glass door was a girl with a pixie cut, blue jeans, and a checkered flannel shirt. The first time I saw her, three months ago, she was a human lamp, wearing nothing but a fez.

"Dawn—"

"Hello, Mr. Fuller—"

"Dispense with the formalities, Dawn. You can call me, Hayden."

She smiled awkwardly, her teeth denting her lower lip.

I unlocked the door and let her in. I wondered why, in this humidity, she was wearing a long-sleeved shirt.

"I know it, but the AC inside offices—"

"Obviously. You've never been in my office." I flipped on a desk fan and opened a window. Traffic from Yonge Street bled into the room. "AC? I don't even have plush chairs."

She slid into a wooden chair and quickly propped her elbows on my desk blotter and smiled across from me. Small specks of lipstick marked her teeth. I tossed my porkpie toward the hat rack in the near corner, behind the door, and it bounced off a stem and to the floor. I tossed it a second time, hit the target on a third. "I'm no James Bond."

She laughed.

People don't always get my jokes. I like it when they do.

I too sat down. "What can I do for you?"

Since my last case, I heard she was turning her life around, no longer ushering at Maple Leaf Gardens as a page girl. She was taking correspondence courses toward her GED and working at the downtown Eaton's. Toy department. "You look good," I said, trying to keep my eyes on hers.

She smiled. "You look tired. You must be working on a case."

"I am."

"Bobby Ehle?"

"Yeah."

Wrinkles formed at the corners of her eyes and her voice was a rush of worries. Bobby Ehle was her boyfriend, and he skipped out, not because he killed Nancy, but because he was running from the mob. They wanted to kill him for a bad drug deal. "You see, Mr. Fuller, I was making a delivery for a Dr. Airedale, well actually his associate Dr. Williams. Well, I was making it for Bobby. He was feeling sick and—"

"Slow down. Who's Dr. Williams?"

Gillian Williams was another plastic surgeon who co-owned and performed out-patient surgeries and hydrotherapy sessions at Adora Borealis, the Queen Street clinic. Her specialties: breast reduction, tummy tucks, and face lifts.

"Adora Borealis." I laughed.

It was such a cornball name.

"You want to know the real kicker." She smiled. It's ad slogan was "the Northern Lights of Beauty."

That just cracked me up. It was tastelessly Canadian.

"So Dr. Williams sent you on a drug run? You sure?"

"I think so. I don't know. I didn't look in the canisters." It was a long train ride from Toronto to Montreal. Three canisters in a suitcase. She saw the canisters placed there. Bobby placed them there. She repeated how she never looked in the canisters.

"Bobby was too sick?"

"Yeah. Sometimes he gets—" She looked away and bit at one of the corners of her shirt collar.

Outside the traffic chatted like folks in a theater lobby, between acts, smoking cigs. A jackhammer mildly thudded, and rock music climbed up from a passing hack that had its windows lowered. A street vendor shouted the day's headlines. Something to do with de Gaulle and his take on Expo '67. A wasted extravagance. Quebec for Quebecois. I closed the window.

"I didn't look in the suitcase. But it must have been drugs." Anyway, the drop happened and the real shipment wasn't delivered. They, the folks on the other end, never got what they asked for, whatever that was, "but I figured it was drugs. I mean, I didn't know what it was at the time, but I was getting a hundred for the delivery, and what else could it have been?"

Blueprints for a new a new hydrogen bomb, body parts packed in ice, vials full of flesh eating viruses? I mean, come on, this case had taken a weird turn once LSD Blue 27 was thrown into the gumbo.

"Slow down." I leaned forward. The light from the street was an amber glare that had Dawn shielding her eyes. "Gillian Williams, directly, she, asked you to do this?"

I wondered about Williams's possible involvement with LSD Blue 27.

"Well not directly. Bobby was in contact with Gillian, I think, and asked me to make the drop for him and I traveled the train." Dawn blinked her green eyes. There was a flaw in one of them, a slight scythe in an iris, resembling a floating eye lash. I wondered why I'd never noticed it before.

"But you never saw Dr. Williams or Dr. Airedale handling the canisters?"

"No."

"And Bobby was too sick to make the delivery himself?"

Sometimes the meds make him immobile. He can't even get out of the apartment or change the channel on the TV.

"Does he work?"

"Construction. Occasionally. This week. Construction."

"Uh-huh." I doodled on my desk blotter. A hockey net, gloves, a puck. "Who was on the other end? Of the drop?"

"Some guys, wise guys I think." She smiled nonchalantly. The touches of red lipstick that daubed her teeth were distracting, strangely sexy. I kept telling myself I was thirty.

When not leaving lipstick accents on her teeth, Dawn chewed on the triangle tip of one of the ends of her collar. She was such a kid. No wonder she and Bobby connected so well.

"What did they look like?"

Sharp chins, lean faces, gloves on their hands. Wise guys, you know?

"Yup. Sounds like wise guys. And they say they didn't get what they were supposed to get?"

"Yeah. One of them was kind of bookish. Wore a black lamb-skin hat and very mod clothes."

"Did you get his name?"

"Dennis. Well, Denys. He's French."

"I figured that."

She smiled and shook her head, slightly embarrassed. "He also had a birthmark, like a club, like in a deck of cards—"

"A three-leaf clover?"

"Yeah."

"It wasn't a tattoo?"

"It might have been. But who gets one on their face?" The marking was under his left eye, and almost looked like three tears.

"Maybe it wasn't a clover, but tears?"

"Maybe." She gently tugged on the gold necklace around her neck. It was a gift from Bobby.

Tears. Crying over what? And what was a nice girl like Dawn doing with a lost soul like Bobby Ehle, a lost soul who couldn't even change the channels on his television? "It could be a double-cross. They're lying. Or, Bobby made the switch before you boarded the train."

"No. He wouldn't do that. He loves me." She couldn't look at me. The amber lights of Yonge Street were bright but not that bright. She played with a crease line in her jeans. The jackhammer, with the window closed, had become a dull pound. "He wouldn't set me up."

"Oh, he wouldn't would he?" I'd seen some nasty photographs authored by my virtuous client.

"No, he wouldn't." The crease on her jeans must have been a thin creek by now, the way she was working it. Soon it would be a river.

She absently looked up at me, smiled weakly, and edged at the crease more furiously, and then pounded her leg with a closed fist, the rhythm of her hits in step with the jackhammer outside.

"Your leg okay?"

"When I get nervous or stressed it twitches. Throbs." It starts with a thin tremble, then starts throbbing. "Bobby, double-cross me?"

She tried trapping tears behind her mouth, and then her voice was full of them. "It's not like that—"

"He's a desperate man. He may have killed his wife."

"I don't believe that either—"

"Uh-huh."

"You don't believe me?"

"No, that's not it, Dawn." I smiled. "I just like saying 'uh-huh' when I get stressed."

That made her smile and laugh. It was a little wet.

This was the first time I had heard of Bobby's great love for Dawn. He hadn't even mentioned her at my house. I reached for her hand. Her fingers were strong. And like her leg, trembling. "How long you two been dating?"

"Two months." She unclasped the gold chain from around her neck. It looked a little dusky and lumpy in my hands. "That's a friendship bracelet," she said.

It was gold-plated. Their anniversary was last Friday, the day before Bobby may have killed Nancy. She shrugged. They ate an anniversary meal at Bassel's. Had hamburgers. "It's a nice restaurant."

"Yeah, I know. I've been there," I said.

She had never dated a man for more than two weeks before. This felt different. Like when you really care, like really really care.

I nodded and handed her back her necklace. A fleck or two of gold dust slivered my fingers. "And when did this drop not happen?"

"Three days ago. And now the mob's trying to kill me. Well, Bobby, mainly. But I'm his accomplice. Everywhere I go. I can't—" She struggled with the clasp and asked me to snap it back in place. Her hair smelled of flowers.

Like the other day at the R.O.M., for instance—she goes there to relax and write poems—anyway, she felt she was being followed. There was this real creepy guy, tall, and heavy set with a jaunty little bowler on his head.

"A lot of people go to the R.O.M. Not all of them to write poems." I smiled. "Dinosaurs are popular with the kids these days."

"I know, but this one guy, he was creepy. A girl knows all about creepy looks, you know? He was slinking along the fern plants. Following, watching me. It felt like he was touching my tits with his eyes."

It surprised me how quickly she could move from innocent

ingénue to tough-talking dame.

"I'm sorry I shouldn't have said tits. But I guarantee you that he knew my measurements and cup size."

"Sure, sure." I think I was blushing a little. 34B.

And his face, Mr. Fuller, was real tight.

"Like it's wrapped in Saran Wrap?" Jack Palance without the black vest and fringe and Shane giving him hell.

"Yes. Like Jack Palance."

She sure knew her movies.

Athol Leighton. Cool Athol, ex-NHL'er and Babe Migano's hit man. "Where else you seen him?"

"Yesterday. On King Street. The cigar store." She looked away. "I lost him on the subway exchange."

"Athol Leighton is his name."

"Asshole? Really?"

I laughed. "Athol. A-T-H-O-L. It's British. But Asshole fits." I laughed again. "Yeah. It fits real fine." I doodled across my blotter, a smiley face, a circle with a dot in the middle, a maple leaf, a horse. I draw terrible horses. Mine always look like a drunken moose. What was I going to do with Dawn? She needed protection, but I couldn't take her on a case this hot. And it was going to get a lot hotter.

Athol Leighton meant Babe Migano, the ex-Montreal kingpin and now Toronto-area gangster, was thrown into this criminal gumbo with its domestic violence, LSD Blue 27, and unsavory plastic surgeons. Migano said he had wanted to go legit, open a chain of restaurants, get in the good, fast money, but perhaps the drug part of this case, LSD Blue 27, was too enticing a piece of the action to cut himself out of. "You saw Bobby before you boarded the train? He gave you the package?"

She nodded. "Packages. They were in these cylinders. They looked like they'd hold lenses for a camera or something. Long lenses."

"Uh-huh."

The phone on my desk rang. I apologized and answered. Stana.

"Terry Quniton. He's the pilot. You were on the right rack with KEY. He didn't report to CKEY this morning. You know, 590 on your dial? Everyone's doing traffic reports these days. He does their traffic report. Helicopters."

"He call in sick?"

"No. Nothing."

"Shit, Stana. Thanks. I appreciate this."

"The dispatcher says that two days ago she saw him talking to a fella that fits Bobby's description."

"Wow."

"He's probably the one, huh?" She paused. I heard her pencil clack-clacking against the mouthpiece of the phone. "I'm in. I'll help—"

"Thanks. I got a client. We'll talk."

"Sure. And happy birthday. Thirty, huh?"

"Yeah. I'm no longer the same age as Clark Kent."

"I'll call you later, Superman."

"Thanks, Lois." I placed the receiver on its holder.

"Terry, huh?" The line on Dawn's forehead, between her eyebrows creased, resembling the fold in a daily.

"You know him, Dawn?"

"Yeah. He's Bobby's friend. They grew up in Montreal together. Watched hockey at our place, Saturdays—"

Bobby called him a fucko, said fucko was fucking his ex.

Her eyes wandered, her mind shifting to something she should have recalled earlier. Terry has a tattoo on his left shoulder, a fleur-de-lis. One time he was in a T-shirt, drinking beers, and she asked him about it. It looks a bit like the clover on Denys's face, she said.

"You think the clover might be a fleur-de-lis?"

"Maybe. A fleur-de-lis that's crying?" Denys's version sure looked like tears.

"Interesting."

"It was definitely crying." She smiled, pleased.

I tapped my fingers on the blotter. "You ever hear of LSD Blue 27? Did Bobby ever say anything about that?"

He did. And it wasn't LSD Blue 27, Mr. Fuller. Just Blue 27. That's what it was called on the streets.

"There's a lot of this on the street?"

"Some."

Bobby was taking it, but it wasn't helping that much. At first it made the headaches go away but then it started making him forget things and, well, she didn't really want to talk about it, but in bed, it made it difficult for him to get intimate, you know, like all the desire was gone. He couldn't stay—

"Interested?"

"Yeah. That's a good way to put it, Mr. Fuller. *Interested.*" And he hated not being his old self and, you know, that's important with men, the whole proving yourself in bed thing.

"Yeah." I smiled absently. I was no MVP in the bedroom.

Anyway, he started putting on weight, and that frustrated him even more. He refused to get new jeans, cramming himself into the old ones, his belt tighter and tighter around his waist, trying to hitch his pants in place. And, Mr. Fuller, he sought out other solutions, too, for the weight, eating only one meal before supper, a can of soup, and for the headaches, hydrotherapy. Electric shock.

"When did he last take the blue pills?"

"Off and on. I'm not sure he ever stopped. He just cut back. Tried other things." She looked away. "I mean the headaches were so bad."

"Yeah." I rubbed the edge of my chin. "Did he ever hit you?"

"No, no. Never. He never even got mad. Ever. If anything I'd like to have seen him get mad—"

"No you wouldn't."

I didn't want any woman to ever look like Nancy again, hair

missing from the left side of her head, just over an ear. A faded human carpet.

"Well, I just mean in terms of sexual energy." They had even tried incense, rare resins from Mexican plants, special oils at the back of his neck, and fondue. I'm not sure how melted cheese would help, but Bobby was a big fan. Anyway, Dawn said that the blue pills transformed Bobby into that old tom cat, you know the one you wait too long to fix, and then when you do he just sits on top of the TV and stares at you?

That just cracked me up. I really shouldn't have been laughing but she didn't seem to mind.

I wondered if she'd ever gone to the clinic, the Northern Lights of Beauty, what did it look like on the inside? "What was the setup?"

"Small staff. Two or three nurses. Three doctors."

"Three?"

"There's Stangl. Alex Stangl. He works in the lab." She shrugged. There's also a lot of white rooms, she said. The hydrotherapy room was all white: walls, tile, and long angular windows with bars on it. The bars were even painted white. Bobby would rest there, covered in some kind of hydro blankets, earphones on his head, listening to jazz music, while the water around him pulsed and pushed and rippled and did whatever hydrotherapy does.

"You don't believe in it?"

"Was you ever bit by a dead bee?"

Another movie reference. And a pretty good one at that.

"Anything else you saw?"

A lab in back straight out of those freaky Frankenstein films with beakers and Bunsen burners, test tubes, vials, scales, and machines with a lot of lights. Green lights and red. And rooms, like hotel suites for overnight clients.

"Bobby ever stay overnight?"

"Sure. Lots of times." She stayed with him three or four times.

They were given filtered water. Told to drink it. A lot of water.

"Filtered water?"

"Purity to fight the body's impurities. They were big on that. Lots of filtered water, 24–7."

"He *never* hit you?"

"Never."

But he might have double-crossed her. The diamond necklace he got Dawn was straight out of a Crackerjack box. Goddamn four-flusher. I didn't tell her that but sure as hell wanted to.

"He's probably in Sweden, huh? You think Terry went too?"

"I'm not sure."

"There's one other thing. One time I was at Adora Borealis, like last week, with Bobby and I saw him. A man no-one has seen for weeks. Months."

"Who?"

"Brian 'Spinner' Terrien."

The back of my neck and arms tingled. *Spinner was dead. I saw him die.*

I didn't repeat this aloud to Dawn. At least I don't think I did.

She read my incredulity, however. It was him, she insisted. The angular shoulders. The walk. She had seen him plenty of times at the Gardens during his up-and-down playing days. He was living in one of the back rooms at the clinic. She said hello, but he hesitated, smiled briefly and slunk away to an adjoining room. She leaned forward. "It was the same hair from his playing days, looked like—"

"A Brillo pad?"

"Yeah. A Brillo pad. It's like he's hiding out there or something."

"Or something." How long ago was this?

The last time Bobby got a treatment. Three days ago.

Spinner died in a garage, one of his eyes hanging away from the orbital bone, resting against a cheek as intermittent bubblegum bursts of blood puffed from his lips.

"Will you protect me?" She didn't have much money but she didn't know where else to turn. Her father was dead and her mother wanted nothing to do with her. *Like I said before, it always comes down to trouble with the fathers doesn't it?*

And me trapped in a suitcase full of drying moths.

I got on the blower. Dr. Abramowitz, a good friend of mine out in the north-end suburbs. He took care of me and my concussions during my playing days and has ever since. He asked if I were having any dizzy spells and I lied, said I was fine, and then told him the whole story, the death threats, and Athol Leighton, and Bobby Ehle wanted for murder, and he said sure, bring the girl over. Oh, and he said one other thing, "Slow down kid."

It was a standing joke between us. He knew I only had one gear and it was revving in fifth. I'd bring the girl over in the next hour or so. I smiled at Dawn. "How much you have?"

She reached into her back pocket for a tiny pink wallet. It took her a while to get it out of her back pocket. Her jeans were tight. Youth. "Fifty?"

"Give it to me."

She did.

I handed her back all of it but two tens.

"That's the amount you gave me three months ago." She smiled. "That time in Cal Bullard's office and I was a human lamp."

"How old are you, Dawn?"

"Twenty. I turned twenty last week—"

Bobby was thirty-something. I was thirty.

I needed a girlfriend, age appropriate, of course.

"I know what you're thinking. I'm too young to know what love is, but I love him, Mr. Fuller." She didn't know how to explain it—it was just a part of her like breathing or waking or walking. You don't think about it, you do it. You love.

I had felt that way too, once, back in 1962–64, with Stana.

Christ that was some time ago. Back then I smiled all the time.

"It hurts to love the way I love." She looked down at her leg and tapped her thigh's tremors. They were ebbing, becoming a trickle. "Shit, sometimes I wonder if I'll ever grow up." She felt like a kid, needing help reaching for the damn glasses on the top shelf of the kitchen cabinet.

"I keep asking myself that question too." There was so much I didn't know and the older I got the more I realized it.

She smiled and it filled her green eyes, turning teal from the amber light off Yonge Street. "The whole life experience thing—sucks."

"It gets easier."

"Really?"

"No." I smiled and laughed at my previous lie. "I wish it were true."

We both shrugged.

"I guess we're even now." She crossed one leg over the other.

"I guess so."

"I mean I'm returning the twenty." The smile that had stretched to her eyes now flowed through her, all the way to her hands and fingertips. She was no longer trembling. "I can cook for Dr. Abramowitz. I can. Well not much. Eggs, pasta, peanut butter and jelly—"

"That's not cooking. Peanut butter and jelly's not cooking."

"With a glass of milk it's a complete meal. Especially if you use whole-wheat bread."

I gave her a doubtful look. "He'll order out. I'll pay him. And I'll see if I can straighten things out about Athol with Babe Migano."

"Did you know Bobby was selling hockey sticks in back of the Gardens to get by?" She shifted in her chair. The sun was now a bar across her shoulders and chest. One of the triangles to her collar was a darker color than the rest of the shirt. The jackhammer was still quietly pounding. "He had no money left from his hockey days and being too tired to work construction was selling broken practice sticks, autographing them for the fans."

I nodded. Bobby would be in Sweden soon. What was in those damn canisters? My money was on Blue 27. Or maybe something more potent, something cooked up in Airedale and Williams's lab on Queen Street, the Adora Borealis.

The Northern Lights of Beauty.

Give me a fucking break.

4

Something didn't feel right as soon as we hit Yonge Street. There was a crew crushing up concrete, but the technique of the main guy jackhammering the sidewalk was all wrong. He was using a lift assist, but the way he hovered, with his full belly over the jackhammer's handles, didn't allow the lift assist to do much assisting. I had an uncle who could not only change light switches but worked construction and he always said keep a safe distant from you and the jackhammer, the list on the left hand side, and allow it to make you more efficient. Sure this guy had a lot of fat and muscle, torqueing up shards of road, but it was all misplaced energy.

And then there was his hard hat. It didn't quite fit his head. It was too loose and rode up in front like a springboard, like he was more concerned with getting face time in a W.W. II action film than just doing his job. The fella next to him was even more wrong. He was holding a paper bag. A typical Yonge Street rummy, with his early afternoon shadow, crumpled sport jacket, and stained khakis, but the shoes, the damn shoes. Too clean. Not quite business casual but too damn new. Always start with the shoes when building a character, an actor friend once told me, and these fellas knew nothing about character.

Dawn was saying something or other about mac and cheese and how most people made it with sharp cheddar but the key ingredient was the hard yellow cheese, gruyere, from Switzerland,

and she could whip that up for Dr. A, damn straight she could, she'd forgotten how good she was at making that dish, and I said swell, thinking about peanut butter and jelly and the guy's belly over the jackhammer handles, and how he seemed to bury the bit too deeply into the ground, when Skid Row reached inside his crumpled bag for something other than a mickey.

That's when I reached for my snub-nosed.

The black checkered grip of his gun peeked over the bag's lip, but my. 38 was already barking.

The first shot hit him in the cheek and his mouth wobbled like a wave. The second broke off a whole set of front teeth and he stumbled and fell and choked and died, gray matter and grits of bone on the sidewalk. The crumpled bag was at his feet, the gun still gripped in his left hand.

I quickly shoved Dawn aside, sending her to the curb's edge and into an adjacent parking meter as I waited for the other fella to reach behind his belt for a hidden gun, but he came at me instead with the damn jackhammer, stabbing at my legs, blasting up bits of concrete around my feet, forcing me to fall back on my ass.

I never could dance.

And my elbows were sore as hell.

And then dumbass tried to bore a hole through my belly.

I avoided the bit, twisting left, then right, before firing into his belly. Three rapid knocks. He fell hard, writhing, bouncing a little, his body the shape of the letter C.

A gut-shot is not a nice way to checkout of a building.

He was moaning, his voice the sound of a small dog with a broken leg. His moans slid into seven or eight Hail Marys.

I hoped he had enough left to hold on until the ambulance arrived.

He didn't. I smelled shit.

Workers crowded around us, one guy, in a cut-off gray sweatshirt, acted like he was going to make trouble, but I flashed my

P.I. license and gave him a surly snarl, Kirk Douglas on bennies, shouting these guys are Lenny Cassel's hitmen, and he backed off.

Dawn called the police from a nearby Beckers, and then we sat on the sidewalk and waited and waited for Sal Lambertino.

Dawn didn't scream or yell. I was surprised at how cool she was.

She kissed my cheek, hair smelling of flowers.

I guess I had saved her life.

"That's not Athol," she said.

"No, that's not Athol."

"Neither's the other one."

"Nope."

People crowding around us kept their distance. The guy in the cut-off grays had his hands on his hips, eyes focused. On me. They were full of black flies.

I looked at the flaw in Dawn's iris, the tiny scythe, and wanted to kiss her. I did. The gun never left my hand.

THEY WERE DETROIT-AREA mobsters. Johnny "Red Eye" Thompson, nicknamed for his penchant in delivering late night hits, was the guy with no front teeth. He was a handsome guy at one time: blond hair, big teeth, cleft in his chin, a regular playboy. I bet he slept in a circular bed. The other cat was Danny "Lazy Legs" Langois. Buzz cut, aquiline nose, eyes too closely set. Both were on their way to the morgue in the basement of Wellesley hospital.

At least I hear it's air-conditioned.

"Cassel muscle no doubt about it," Sal said, rubbing at his Hemingway beard. It had just come in over his radio. Rap sheets as long as a city block. "Jesus Christ, cowboy, you're getting a little too good at this killing thing. Three is it now?"

I don't think Clarence S. Campbell will be inviting me back into the NHL anytime soon.

I shielded the sun from my eyes. The tips of my shoulders hurt. I wondered who Johnny Jackhammer replaced on the construction crew. The teamsters are unionized. You don't just step onto a crew. Even if you have Cassel credentials. Somebody didn't check into work today. Let's follow up that thread and find that somebody.

"That's a pretty big hunch."

"I know, I know." This from the man who can't fix a light switch. "How else did Thompson become a member of that crew, on this day?"

Sal barked into the microphone snaking around his rearview mirror, telling them to check into the list of workers on that particular crew. He rubbed at the top of his sandy-hair head. Like me he sported a buzz cut. We were a couple of 1950s cats adrift in the 1960s. You'll never catch either of us in Nehru jackets.

"I'm no cowboy, Sal. They never gave me a choice." I shrugged. Shit, I really wanted to bowl a few more frames or listen to some jazz to calm the edge off my shoulders and arms. My trigger hand still trembled. Dexter Gordon, Hank Mobley, Freddie Hubbard. Those cats could help, right about now, take the tremble out of me. Calm me.

"They really gave Hayden no chance," Dawn echoed, her long legs crossing their way to the street's edge. We were doing the initial interview right here on Yonge, the sun a sharp edge of light.

Dawn was in the clear, after she told her story of the drop gone wrong. She wasn't seen as an accessory nor was Sal sizing her up for any criminal misdemeanors or felonies. She truly didn't know what was in the canisters and he believed her. I think he felt a little sorry for how she was all mixed up with a wrong guy like Bobby Ehle. And that pixie cut and green eyes. With a flaw in the iris. Who could resist that?

I reminded myself I was thirty, repeat thirty.

When it came my turn to talk, I wasn't getting any Dawn

treatment, go for a skate, kid, uh-uh. Sal thought I was just a tool, not thinking straight. "The guy's a fucking lowlife," he mumbled, when Dawn's shoulders were turned.

But we weren't done with the interviews. Sal wanted us to go downtown to make a full report, and, no, we couldn't get a warrant issued to Airedale and Williams's clinic. There just wasn't enough evidence.

"What do we need for crissakes?" Dawn was terse, impatient.

He turned to Dawn. "Did you ever see these two killers at the clinic?"

She shook her head dejectedly.

"Did you ever see them or Dr. Williams or Dr. Airedale involved with LSD Blue 27?" He pushed back his gray fedora and dropped his hands on his hips.

"Blue 27," Dawn corrected. The only stranger Dawn had ever seen at the clinic was one Brian Spinner Terrien, five eight, 145 pounds. Hair sharp like a Brillo pad. The same Spinner I and Migano and Stana and a few others knew had said the long goodbye long ago and was buried in rolls of black dirt out in a field near Vaughan, Ontario.

Okay, Sal said, even if Dawn saw Spinner that wasn't enough grounds for a warrant. He's not wanted or connected to any crime.

I nodded. *No, he's not wanted for much of anything but a decent burial.*

"The guy's probably taking a respite."

Some respite.

More squawk on the call box. Sal ducked his head through the passenger window to listen.

Drugs cost money. Street money. Junk like Blue 27 isn't covered by Canada's HIDS Acts Program. It's not part of universal health care. How much was this junk costing him? Did he ever write a check?

"What are you babbling about?" Sal returned from the recesses of his car, a '65 Ford Falcon. One of the hubcaps was missing.

There I was doing it again. Talking out loud. A by-product of hockey concussions. "Bobby was taking a lot of those blue pills. They cost money. Look into his bank accounts. See if he routinely wrote checks, big checks to Airedale and Williams." If he did, and I was betting on it, and if they can't account for large sums of money brought in from a poor, destitute ex-hockey player, then we probably have reasonable and probable grounds to go in and search the joint.

The Adora Borealis. The Northern Lights of Beauty. Flop house for fallen stars.

"I'll get my people on it."

I waved my hand, flashing away the frayed edges of sun, and that's when I realized the sun wasn't that bright. There was a pain cluttering behind my eyes, in my head, spun cotton candy. When Lazy Legs bounced me to the sidewalk it jarred my neck and back enough to trigger a post-concussive aftershock. I stared down at my shoes and felt dizzy. Shit. So, I moved to the shade of an awning. A lot of fucking good that did.

"Can you get anymore fucking pretentious than Adora Borealis," Sal philosophized.

"The Northern Lights of Beauty," Dawn joined in, arms comically stretched wide like Julie Andrews singing in the mountains.

"Stop." I'm not big on musicals. People knowing words to songs they're singing for the first time. What's with that?

Sal laughed. "Yeah, what is with that," he said. "And remember. Just don't go all cowboy again." He pointed a finger at me. This had become his new signature move since he traded in his police man blues for Sloan Wilson grays. "You got no jurisdiction there."

"I know, Sal, just conversations. Dean Martin style. I'll keep it light."

His eyes creased and his upper lip trembled slightly. "Uh-huh."

That cracked me up. First Jack Webb and now a killer impression of yours truly.

Who knew Sal could be so damn funny.

"The radio call I just got. The other construction worker. The one who didn't check in today?"

"Yeah."

"Bobby Ehle."

AFTER WE FILED our reports at the Bay Street Station, Dawn was taken into police custody for her own protection.

They didn't tell me where they were holding her.

I was worried with her out of the mix, Bobby's contact person was bottled up, denying me, in turn, access to him.

From a street corner, I called Dr. A. and filled him in. Two more people dead. "You sure *you're* all right?" I nodded, but he couldn't see me, and then he asked when was I seeing my therapist? She had called. I had cancelled last Tuesday and Dr. A and her were friends. "Don't skip out again. See her, Hayden."

"Okay, okay."

"I'm not asking—"

The man had such gravitas. He was a Holocaust survivor. So was Dr. Jeanette Cohen, my therapist. You listen to and pay respect to people like that.

I dry swallowed some pills, ate another hotdog, and at 3:45 called Stana from a different drugstore phone, told her what went down outside my office, and asked her to look into any ties Cassel might have with Montreal and Migano. She hesitated, but assured me she was no longer on Migano's payroll, was no longer aces in the kingpin's pocket. "I quit after the death of Spinner and Lisa." I wasn't sure if I could believe her or not. For the time, I decided I'd roll the dice and take the risk. And then I told her about "Terrien" being spotted at the Adora Borealis by Dawn. "He" was hiding in one of the back recovery rooms. Stana's voice caught, and the silence filled the space between us, like the brief pause after a referee blows his whistle and just before he drops the puck.

"But you saw him die—"

I was pretty sure I did. Yes, I had been pistol-whipped into a daze, my head full of Vic's vapor rub, but I saw Spinner quit breathing, I saw the eye hanging from the orbital bone. He was no Lazarus.

"I got a key," she said.

"To the clinic?"

"The Northern Lights of Beauty? Yeah. I have a key." Nancy had given it to her along with some other personal effects she hadn't turned over to the police.

I was going in the front doors, for now. A little conversation. I might need the key later on.

"Right," she said.

Before she signed off she reminded me that a disguise or cover story wouldn't work, they'd recognize me as soon as I walked through their doors. Remember, I'm the ex-Leaf who took photographs of Airedale's baggy ass back when he was fucking Nancy.

"Baggy ass, indeed," I said.

THE OFFICE WAS DARK, a narrow edge of light burning through the slight fissure in the drawn curtains.

I requested it to be that way. Sonny Clark was on the turntable, "Cool Struttin." I requested that too.

I lay on a couch that smelled of wool and fabric softener. One low watt lamp burned next to Dr. Cohen. She had helmeted hair, thick and coarse, and a round face full of a sad optimism. She was fortyish, and leaned back in a swivel chair. Pince-nez glasses propped up along the front of her nose, giving her a distinguished appearance. She looked a bit like Emma Goldman. A tabby cat, with a scratch over its left eye, perched behind her.

The cat was licking a paw, as if removing leftover bits of fish bones. Dr. Cohen really didn't care much for cats, but this one had wandered in out of the rain one day and had chosen to adopt the good doctor. So she took it in. I don't think it had a name.

Dr. Cohen wore a black crepe dress with heavy ruffles in the sleeves and every time she moved in her chair, shifting about, the dress made a sound like bits of tissue paper tearing. Did she ever wear anything but black?

At some of our sessions the roles get kind of reversed and she tells me of the depression she suffers from, the survivor's guilt for being the one still standing. She lost her mother, father, sister and uncle at Dachau. Occasionally, limping with remorse, she finds herself drifting toward the Prince Edward Viaduct, peering down below, and imagining letting go, tumbling, falling through the sky, over and over, never hitting bottom, just forever falling, like tumbling dice, a game of chance. These feelings don't consume her, much, but when they do nudge through her defense mechanisms, they are bright flames, a fallen jet burning in the woods. It's a fight to not become a part of the debris.

After such confessions, she smiles, and in a heavy, full and yet melodic voice praises herself for being so present before me, opening up, allowing the vulnerability to show. Why can't I reciprocate her intimacies with some of my own? That's how it's supposed to work, Hayden. I tell you what hurts me. And then you return the favor. What hurts you?

So I shrug and laugh nervously.

Nothing hurts me. Nothing.

I can't let it hurt me.

So nothing does.

It's like a script, a mantra, I repeat it again and again whenever I start feeling too much or a heavy rain falls. *Water—bathtubs—taffy—*

I shrug a lot during our sessions and talk circles around what's really bothering me, my asshole father. He used to hit me with the belt for mixing his drinks the wrong way. You put the ice in first, then the drink, not the other way around. I never could figure that out. What difference did it make? But when he saw that I didn't remember correctly, the belt came off.

I just can't open up. I can't tell her these things. I believe in being a professional, never whining, doing my job. Punch the clock and do the best you can. No point crying over what I can't change. Let's move on. What am I going to do today and tomorrow? Forget the past. Live in the now.

"There are no clocks here," she often says. "If we have to stay longer, we stay longer. This is not work. This is a free space to express."

And she wanted me to open up, to let go, so that I could live in the present more freely.

I can't let go. I can't open up. And some days I can't even tie my shoes. The headaches.

"Always with the jokes." She shakes her head, her intonation reminding me of Dr. A.

So today, she told me a story, one that I'll never forget. When she was in Dachau, you lose all of your "inner-directedness," your identity, self, living for food, for enough to sustain you through the next minute, hour, day. You're reduced to an animal. One woman, Leah, had been a dancer back in Germany, and she now only looked down at her lap and her flipped up hands. One day, as she and several others were being led to the gas chambers, one of the SS officers, laughed, saying weren't you at one time a dancer. He named the cabaret. Let's see you dance. And she did.

I said nothing.

Was she motivated by other-directed choices, trying to please them? That's what they thought, but as she danced, she pirouetted closer to the officer, removed his gun, and shot him, through the heart. She of course was immediately killed by his fellow officers, but this act was a free act, her last one. Through dancing she had re-claimed a part of her lost identity, her autonomy, her inner-directed self. Isn't that what detective work is for you, a chance to claim your lost autonomy?

"I guess so," I said, not looking at her.

"How are you not free in your everyday life?" *How are you a part of the lonely crowd, guided by the approving nods, commands of others?*

"You're getting kind of theoretical now, aren't you, doc? *Lonely Crowd?*"

"I use a cross-discplinary approach to my work." She smiled tightly. "David Reisman," she mumbled. A sociologist.

Honestly, there are things that I'd like to tell you, doc, but I can't. I just can't. I shrugged. "I really didn't feel anything over the man I killed, the one in the last case."

"Nothing?"

I inhaled wool and fabric softener. The little doilies on the arms and head rests of the couches and chairs must be washed daily. It just smelled too good in here. Reminded me of my grandma's basement. I took in another breath. "No, doc."

"Hayden. Don't call me, doc." She shifted in her chair, tissue paper crinkling. "Call me Jeannette or Dr. Cohen. I have a name. Don't diminish me."

"I'm sorry, Jeannette."

"And what was the name of the man you killed?"

"Johnny "Red Eye" Thompson—a real handsome fucko—"

"Do I detect a note of jealousy?"

"He was one of those made guys, you know? Thought the world was his? Blond hair, capped teeth. Entitlement, you know? Looked like Tab Hunter without a surf board." I was Jewish. I had to fight for everything.

"What about the other one, the other man you killed, the last case?"

She wouldn't say his name. She wanted me to. I wouldn't say it either.

"Iago of the Year Award Winner, 1965. The human toad?"

She wrote something on a yellow note pad. "You can't even acknowledge him."

"What's to acknowledge?"

"Own up to it. He was a human being."

"Was he?" I still wouldn't say his name. I'm a stubborn son of a bitch.

"You told me your father was an alcoholic—"

"Still is."

"Your mother, dead."

"Yes. Died when I was eight." Tears pushed behind my eyes. I wasn't going to show it though.

"Your father used to take you to the bars and keep you parked outside while he threw darts, for how long, two-three hours?" She flipped pages, her notebook resembling a yellow sand dune. "Three hours, I wrote down, three. How did that make you feel?" She removed her glasses and massaged the two little dents, mini-Frankenstein feet, at the edges of her nose.

"How the fuck do you think it made me feel?"

The gap in the curtain seemed narrower.

"You're still angry."

"Damn right."

I breathed in fabric softener.

"Was some of that anger being transferred to the—"

I sat up in the couch, rocks breaking in my stomach. "What are you saying? That when I killed that man, blew away his brains, I was really killing my own father?"

"I'm suggesting maybe it was a free act—a response to something else—" She smiled and wiped dust off a sleeve of her dress. "Maybe we're dwelling too much in the past. You obviously have a lot of feelings trapped inside you, Hayden. And when you're ready to deal with them, you will."

I shrugged.

"You're minimizing again—"

I looked sideways.

"Shrugging is minimizing—it's a default setting keeping real feelings from being expressed. You need to be more present, mindful, aware—"

"My shoulders ache from old hockey injuries so I shrug—"

"Don't bullshit and joke—"

"Sorry."

"So how do we move forward?"

"Forward with what?"

"You? Your life?" She placed her glasses back on. "What can you do now, to ease the pain, to reintegrate—"

"Well, like you said, there's always the next case, that's what keeps me going, the next—"

"So, you find meaning in this kind of work—?" She shifted again, tissue paper creasing.

"Yeah. When I'm helping people like Dawn. Damn right I do. Yeah." And then I told her how after killing those two men, my gun hand shaking so, I just kissed Dawn, not on the cheek either, on the lips, full, in front of all those people, construction workers, bystanders, through traffic. It wasn't a sexual kiss. I didn't want her. Yes, I was attracted to her, but it was a relief, a need, a—

"An affirmation—"

"Yeah." I looked at my shoes. One of the laces was undone.

"An affirmation that you are alive. Like me, you are a survivor."

I hadn't thought of it that way. She fucking scares me sometimes. She can see right into the secrets of my heart. "I guess so. Yeah."

"So you really have it backwards, don't you, Hayden?"

"What?"

"They *help you*. Your clients give you purpose, meaning." She pointed at me, herself. "I'm going to role play, imagine the screen of your mind": My relationship with Stana is over and my life is somewhat empty, but rather than surrender to the void, give in, fall from the Prince Edward Viaduct, forever falling, falling forever, the work gives me hope. The work justifies existence. There are people a lot worse off than I am. I deal with them every day. I may live a lonely existence, but the work bolsters me up, saving me from loneliness's glare and alienation.

"You sure you're not talking about yourself, doc, Jeannette?"

She was all right. I liked how worked up she got trying to help me.

Dr. Cohen smiled and tapped the arm rests of her chair, the notebook nestled in her lap. "I guess I am." She wrote a note, and scribbled some more. "Fuck, I guess I am."

5

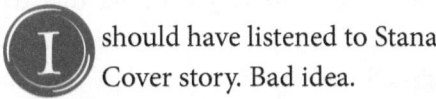 should have listened to Stana.

Cover story. Bad idea.

But I'm stubborn and Airedale was nowhere to be seen and I went with a story that was so covert that the *Spy who Came in from the Cold* cat would want to get tips from me.

Check it: I was Hawley Walker, thorougbred-owning cat, seeking restorative powers for a troubled, ailing mother. Anyway, Dr. Williams, while nodding compassionately over my mother's "plight," sure drank a lot of water. I guess all of the staff at Adora Borealis and their clients did. They were big on that. There were fountains everywhere along the L-shaped building, but Dr. Williams only drank water from the various alcoves, partially hidden recesses. There the water was filtered. And in pitchers. Water was the key to hydration and beauty, it removed all of the poisons from your system. It is the first step to better health.

"Uh-huh," I said, or something equally unimpressed. I'm a bit of a smart-ass.

But she sure was pretty, a surreal beauty. I couldn't look at her directly for fear of being caught staring, breaking professional protocols, so I would catch furtive glances, every now and then, taking in her thin those, the blue eyes set wide apart, and the skin, fresh-scrubbed, porcelain smooth. She had alert eyes, listening to all. Her breathing was steady, calm, natural.

You couldn't hear much of anything else going on in the clinic: few clients, few staff. Adora Borealis was fairly empty. I guess it was 5:46, close to closing time. I had no idea what was going on behind adjacent doors, but one woman, in the lobby, was finishing up with some kind of facial, restorative treatment, her face caked with muddy cream. She was about twenty-seven and like all women in no need of that junk.

We began my "tour" for my troubled mother in the lab. White walls, blue composite counters, and white shelving full of beakers, bottles, test tubes, vials. There were scales that resembled Hobarts right out of the Stabulas's corner store grocery. Microscopes and petri dishes. Bunsen burners. I felt like I was back in eleventh-grade chemistry, dying to get to English class. In case you haven't guessed, I hated chemistry. Never could get the results to the various experiments that I was supposed to get. My litmus paper always turned red when it was supposed to turn blue.

The latter got a laugh out of Dr. Williams. Her voice was husky and her face, when I caught a glimpse refracted in the glass of the cabinet doors, reminded me of a young, platinum blonde Barbara Stanwyck, a combination of expressive eyes and an almost frozen inflexibility. When she spoke, her lips barely moved. They were like the crinkly tied end of a balloon.

A man hunched over a microscope at the far end of the blue counter. He was fiftyish, bald, his eyes when he looked in my direction where a sharp, inviting hazel. Dr. Alex Stangl. He was working the cosmetics end for Adora, perfecting new facial creams.

"I thought you performed surgeries. Plastic—"

"Well we're expanding our base of operations to include cosmetics. Dr. Stangl's perfecting a blemishing cream for women." And then Gillian leaned forward and whispered in my ear how he was also working on a lubricating gel for post-menopausal women to help them get lubricated during sex. With age, some women struggle. Sex hurts.

It sure does.

My father, after my mother died, wandered the apartment aimlessly singing, "Do not forsake me, O, my darling" from *High Noon*, his voice a plaintive wail, loons on a milky lake. He felt alone and forsaken, but I often wondered if he felt that way when she was alive too? I suspect he did, for my father lived in the sorrowful landscapes of Hank Williams songs.

"The gel warms the body within seconds." She smiled. It had some kind of Brazilian extract, aphrodisiac in its composition.

"Interesting," I said, unsure of what else to say. I wasn't quite sure of why I needed to know this, or why her breath against my ear tickled. It wasn't unpleasant.

Dr. Stangl smiled awkwardly. I don't think Dr. Williams was adept at whispering.

I nodded, and then he peered back into his microscope. He kept both eyes open.

We lingered for a few moments. I picked up two or three beakers, but saw no traces of any kind of powder, Blue 27 or otherwise.

"Shall we go to the hydrotherapy room." It wasn't really a question. Dr. Williams hooked her arm around mine and ushered me from the lab.

She floated as we flowed down the narrow halls, the track lighting bright above us. It made her platinum hair look a little bit green.

"So tell me, what do you miss most about the game?"

My back story or cover, the thoroughbred angle, also involved an ex-hockey player joining the family biz. I loved my handle: Hawley Walker. It sounded English, stuffy, and hoi polloi enough.

"But surely, horses aren't enough, you must miss the game." She leaned ever closer, smelling of Chanel No. 5.

I wasn't sure if hockey was the only game she was talking

about.

"I bet you had a lot of pussy during your playing days."

"I had some women, yes." I looked away and sighed with a shallow cough. "The first breakout pass, I miss that." I smiled awkwardly. The quick pass from your own zone that gets the puck moving up ice and on a counter attack. When you execute that well, there's a kind of simplicity and poetry to it. Don't hold the puck long. Look up, and stick to stick, get it to a man who is moving. Don't pass it to a man standing still. Too easy to get it taken away by their forwards. Look for the man moving. "Stuff like that, I guess. It's simple but smart hockey. I miss rituals, the unwritten rules. Hockey has order, you know?"

"Yes." She leaned even closer, bolstering up her arm in mine. One more nudge and she'd be bolstering forth in my back pocket.

I couldn't help but think of her breath in my ear.

"And you like that?"

"Yeah. Who wouldn't?" So much in hockey makes sense.

She was ethereal, that's for sure. We floated further down that hall. Her steps were like curtain edges lifting gently in a slightly open window. I'm a product of the 1950s. I like curvy women with an ample bust line and big hips, and Dr. Williams may have been very petite, her breasts slight, her hands and feet small, but I found her and her fresh-scrubbed face strangely attractive. There wasn't a blemish, a line, a crow's foot, anywhere.

And if you looked long enough you felt like you might catch a reflection of your own face in the porcelain glow of hers.

She had to be mid-to late thirties. She looked twenty-five. Next to her, with my slight scars from 55 stitches, hockey fights, I was Methuselah.

"Howe or Richard?" Her blond hair glowed a shade of green.

"What?"

"Who's the greatest player of all time, Howe or Richard?"

"Is this a test of some kind?"

"Howe or Richard?"

"Doug Harvey." I loved puck-rushing defensemen.

"Doug Harvey?" She laughed. "Well that's outside the box."

"Montreal doesn't win all those cups without Harvey." Seven-time Norris trophy champion. But between Richard and Howe, I had to go with Richard, even though he had retired in 1960 and Howe was still playing, the Rocket was the best money player ever. Over 80 playoff goals, multiple overtime winners, and from the blue line in he was the fastest to the net I'd ever seen. "Richard, no doubt."

I always thought Howe was a bit of a doofus. For years he kept all of our salaries low because he allowed himself to be underpaid. My rookie season, I had been a member of Ted Lindsay's Players Association seeking a fair cut of the profits the owners were raking in with their TV money, watered-down pop, and season ticket prices, and hoarding from us. Lindsay played the game the way I did, tough in the corners, gritty, but he scored a helluva lot more goals, much much more. Next to Claude Provost of the Canadiens, he was my idol.

She stopped. "I'm surprised. I thought you'd say Howe."

"Because I'm English?" Now I figured out the subtle off-Ontario accent. She was French, something about the "e-u" sound in her yous.

"Yeah."

"I'm not, I'm a Jew."

She nodded.

"Besides, lots of English Canadians love Richard. His nickname is English after all. The Rocket. He's not known as La Fusée."

She tapped her chin. "You're right. That's a good point." Her blue eyes glinted with a dusky veil. "Dormiras tu avec moi?"

"I know what that means, doctor."

She laughed, parts of her lower teeth showing. "Of course, you do." Her voice sounded as if she smoked a pack of cigarettes an hour.

I wasn't sure of what to make of all of her overtures.

The expanse of her eyes probably gave her great peripheral vision and created a boundary line between the sublimely stunning pushing up against the edges of the slightly profane. A couple of genetic tweaks and her brittle porcelain mask would crack, fall, to the other side of the beauty equation. It was a surreal balance between the known and oblivion.

And yet, I couldn't stop looking at her, furtive glances and all. Hell, she needed to be on a poster for Oil of Olay.

"You're French, I gather?"

"Oui." She came to Toronto two or three years ago and opened this office with Cliff in 1963. She missed Montreal. Nobody could make croissants like the French, and she thought the architecture of T.O. sucked, bland, too many straight lines and arches, too much Presbyterian righteousness to everything. Boring complacency.

"What about the new City Hall they're building?" It was just a few blocks down from her office and set to be inaugurated soon.

"Just fine, but who landed the spaceship in the middle of it?"

I really didn't know what to say to that.

Dawn sure was right about the joint's whiteness. Everything in this L-shaped compound was a radioactive glow, a full on glare. The walls, the tiles, even her very short lab coat, slacks and shoes. White.

I felt like a slalom racer fighting the snow blind.

Dr. Williams drank more water at one of the many stations along our tour. "You should have some—"

"Uh-huh."

"It's not poison."

I laughed. "It just isn't for me, Dr. Williams. I mean I like water and all but I don't need a drink every ten minutes."

"Call me Gillian."

I liked the name. "Gillian." In my playing days, doc, we were taught to eat steaks before puck drop and *spit out* the water we drank *during* the game. Don't want to get waterlogged.

That' s ridiculous, you need water to replenish. Hockey players are so barbarian.

I couldn't disagree with that part of her assessment. We are barbarians on the ice, especially when we slip into our third faces, but the whole water fetish felt like some kind of goddamn pagan ritual. Any second, I expected to see someone tossed into a volcano.

I only hoped it wasn't about to be me.

More on my clever cover story: Mom (who in reality died when I was eight—gas-oven type suicide) had been in a terrible car accident and was in need of care, the kind of hydrotherapy I hear Adora Borealis specializes in. She gets these terrible headaches.

Hence the tour, the lab, the first-name basis bit. The comical flirting. The whisper in the ear. The pleasant Dr. Stangl overhearing but acting like he didn't. Yet despite the friendly hijinks, Gillian wouldn't let me see what was behind door number one, two, or three. There wasn't even a curtain with Carol Merril.

Clients. Privacy, you know, Dr. Williams said, and we were now floating through some large white doors, the handle looking like one of those wheels that closes a hatch on a submarine.

It too was white. Bleached, bone dry, brighter than chalk.

The hydrotherapy room on the other side glowed like phosphorous.

It was a strange room. The building itself was one story, but this room was two, possibly two and a half stories high.

Even the bars on the windows glowed, just like Dawn said.

I wish I had worn sunglasses.

To the left, high on the wall, ran blocks of glass windows, twelve by twelve with steel reinforcement between them. The glass was tinted and there was probably enough space behind there to host the Toronto Maple Leafs. It reminded me of those hospital dramas on TV where doctors watch other doctors performing surgeries. I waved. Nobody waved back. At least no one I could see.

The room was crammed with tubs and its accompanying accouterments of nozzles and whirlpools and foam guns. A nurse, with one eye higher on her face than the other, greeted us and smiled briefly at me, before looking down at a black lemon scuff mark on her white shoes. She was in her mid-thirties and fleshy in the arms, a little plump. Her face, pale; her hands small. The hair breaking under her white cap was auburn. The violet-colored lipstick she wore made her face even paler, like a member of kabuki theater. I liked her. It was just a feeling I had. I liked her.

"This is Leila. One of our best nurses. She'll probably be working with your mother." Gillian finished introductions, smiled. "She's in charge of our hydrotherapy ward."

We exchanged handshakes. One of Leila's fingers gently pricked my palm like the broken off nub of a rose stem. She looked down once again at the lemon scuff as she prepared to wheel a client away.

"When you're done with her, you're free to go Leila."

"Thank-you, Dr. Williams." Her voice rose from the bottom of a tunnel.

The client, fiftyish, was in a one-piece swimsuit, her knees pointed up, thin hair matting her eyes. She kept nodding her head. At everyone. I said hello. She couldn't stop nodding.

Leila wheeled her away. It wasn't a quiet exit. A wheel caught, over and over again, seemingly screaming, stop, stop.

"You better call CAA and get that thing towed somewhere."

Gillian shook her head, her lips pressing into a thin bemused line. "You have a very good sense of humor, Mr. Walker."

"Thanks. It's part of the new school of comedy, urban smart-ass."

She laughed.

"That gal that left, she okay?"

"Leila can be a little moody—"

"No, I mean the client. With all the nodding and stuff."

"I can't talk about our clients, Hawley."

But she could talk about Leila. Anyway, the Hawley Walker bit was cracking me up. I'm a regular riot all right. *Hawley Walker. Shall we visit any botanical gardens today, luv? Hilarious.*

"Privacy." She smiled sincerely, her face a shiny new coin.

"Of course."

I wondered if the woman with the yen to listlessly nod had been taking too much Blue 27. She sure was lethargic. She nodded in half-time. And that's when I asked Dr. Williams if Dr. Airedale had more radical treatments. I wasn't sure that hydrotherapy would be enough for dear old Mom. The headaches were severe. She was talking tombstones, doc, tombstones, suicide.

Gillian tapped her chin, smiled, and said something reassuring.

I told her about my good friend Bobby Ehle, the cat wanted for murder, and how he told me Dr. Airedale had really helped him out with some kind of experimental treatment involving Blue 27. I made it sound like I really believed in the good doctor, a regular Albert Schweitzer Dr. Airedale was.

Maybe I over played my hand.

"I don't know what you're talking about. Blue 27? This is a place for cosmetic surgery and relaxation therapy, not an episode of *Flash Gordon.*"

I nodded. "I'm just repeating what Bobby told me. Blue 27. Works wonders, he says."

"You should read more racing forms and less comic books, Mr. Walker."

Like I said before—my cover story not a good idea. It hadn't fooled her one bit.

I checked out the switches and levers by the hydrotherapy

tub, looking under the rubber sheets to the nozzles along the side that let out jets of water. This looks cozy, I said, to say something.

I turned the handles, worked the tap trigger. Squeezed. Foam spilled from the gun, like the broken bits of puffed flowers that coated cattails.

"So are you interested in, perhaps, bringing your mother by, to check out the facilities?"

"Sure." I rubbed the sides of my mouth and pushed back my porkpie. "I love the décor. Classy. The white's really attractive. Gives one a sense of hope you know, like the white light you see before checking out, the final taxi? Pearly gates and all? Lots of hope. Love the white."

And then she shrank to another alcove, for another glass of water. She drank quickly, seeking to knock away my humor. One last sip. Gillian never finished any of the glasses. I asked why.

The bottom of the cup, Mr. Fuller, is full of your saliva, your impurities. It doesn't do your body any good to put those *back* in the system. "I never finish my drinks."

She had called me Mr. Fuller. "When did you know?"

"When you walked in." She smiled. "I read the papers. And your hat is a noticeable affectation."

"Affectation?"

Lights flashed above, on the other side of the tinted glass. Our long shadows, resembling narrow birch trees, spread behind me and Gillian. "Yes, asshole, affectation." It was the inestimable Dr. Airedale leaning against the upstairs glass. I recognized his thin voice, even if it were distorted, bleeding and bouncing all over the room through an intercom system he must've purchased for ten dollars at Canadian Tire. He had been tracking the whole conversation, watching with a kind of god-like gaze from above. Mr. Opticon.

"You going to come down here to talk, or do I have to keep looking up, your Highness." My neck was getting sore and I couldn't read his facial expressions. He was a silhouette on glass.

"Fuck you."

More distortion, static over telephone wires.

"Yup, definitely Canadian Tire."

"Go take a flying fuck at a rolling donut—"

"Pithy. I like it. A man of few words. And donuts liven up any party."

He dropped another F-bomb.

"I wasn't inviting an encore." That cracked me up. "Your boys, Airedale, or Cassel's boys, I should say, are dead. Thompson and Lazy Legs? Gone." I snapped my fingers for emphasis. "They're now sleeping the big sleep. Can you pass the message onto Cassel? As in Lenny, Mr. Machete. I think he's just down the hall—an expert in tossing people's remains in trash bags. Your kind of guy."

The upper window lights dimmed back to black.

"I wouldn't push it with him." Gillian leaned closer to me. Her voice was painted with concern, "watch yourself."

"Uh-huh."

"I assure you—" Gillian spoke softly. "There's no Mr. Cassel here." She tapped her chin once or twice, her lips parting while her face appeared immobile.

"Then let me check."

"I can't—"

"Right, right privacy."

"And you don't have a warrant—"

"No. No warrant." I forced a smile. It hurt my face.

She smiled. "I liked blowing in your ear. We should do more of that," she whispered again.

And that's when her hand patted my ass. I have an okay functional ass for a hockey player, helps with power skating, but I was a little embarrassed by the whole deal.

"Come." She had changed her mind. She was going to show me the rooms after all.

There were eight of them, small, nicely furnished. The only one occupied, number five, housed, the woman with the nodding grin. The other seven rooms had no windows, no television, two lamps, a dresser, a small book shelf, a comfortable queen-size bed, blue carpeting, blue walls, a closet, and a private bathroom. Room seven was crammed with pulp novels. I recognized Georges Simenon, Jim Thompson, and Elliott Chaze, *Black Wings has My Angel.* In the bathroom cabinet were several over-the-counter remedies for an upset stomach.

"We haven't cleared this room yet. Our last client left last night."

I wondered if it were Cassel. For a hood he had good reading taste. "Uh-huh," I said. "Who was in here?"

She smiled, her lips barely moving, her blue eyes filling with charm. "An actor. I can't give you his name."

"Is he on a western and says cheerio a lot?"

"I couldn't say." She smiled, the tip of her chin glinting in the low level of light.

Airedale, with a hitch in his walk, huffed into the room, his left leg limping slightly, shifting his body into a wobbly I. "Oh, there you are."

"Here we are," she echoed, her tone mocking, annoyed.

Airedale was very thin, his goatee and hair white, his face sharp angles, ears cuts of pork that didn't fit his narrow face. He wore wool pants and a double-breasted blazer with a crown on the left pocket. He exuded country-club ease, a regular descendent of the United Empire Loyalists.

"Hey, Baggy Ass."

"Fuck you."

"Can't we bring up the level of conversation? I thought doctors appreciated fine wines, abstract art, and discussing the lifetime work of the Durants—she story of civilization series?"

He glared. His face blotchy, mismatched puzzle pieces.

Gillian suppressed a laugh and covered her mouth. "Will and

Ariel, Cliff?"

I guess she had read them too.

He hadn't and that really pissed him off.

We moved out of the room, Cliff getting between the two of us, allowing her to no longer hold forth in my back pocket.

As we crossed white lines of light and tile, Airedale shot her surly looks. She wasn't minding her place. I guess as the senior partner, he was the big Kahuna. "I told you not to fuck with this guy."

And then she laughed, a husky laugh, one that matched her cigarette-tinged voice, and stripped him of his threadbare machismo. "Don't play hardboiled, Cliff. It doesn't suit you. You're no tough guy."

I guess the big Kahuna had suddenly become chum for sharks out in the Pacific.

His eyes sharpened. "I warned you about trying to *play him*."

"Play? I enjoy playing. Playing gives me pleasure. Something I haven't experienced in a long, long time."

I assumed there was some sex stuff going on under all that "play" talk, like telling me all about female lubricant, whispering in my ear, and wondering how much action I got as a hockey player. Maybe Gillian and Cliff were one-time lovers. There was something peevish and petty about their exchanges that suggested a washed-out love that had become swollen apples, falling off trees, crushed under the tread of passing cars.

Maybe they were still fucking. Who knows? For some people, you don't have to be in love to fuck. I'm old-fashioned. That just doesn't fly with me.

Airedale's eyes now filled his voice with blades. "He's a wiseass and we don't need to be amused by him or amuse him. He has no authority here."

He stopped at one of the alcoves and poured himself a drink of water. It was smooth. There wasn't a bubble in it. "Don't give him a chance of using his authority—"

She ignored his outburst, turning politely toward me, assuring me that Bobby Ehle was a client; took hydrotherapy treatments, that's all.

"Can you show me the books, the payments he made?"

She said nothing.

"I think you better be going, asshole." Airedale again, always on point.

"What about dear old Mom? She had such hopes for this place."

"Next time, Gillian, you make a choice to 'entertain' a guest. Consult me—"

"Don't tell me how to behave, Cliff. I don't like it." She crossed arms over her chest. "And I like him, I like Hayden Fuller, and I'd like to see him." She shrugged, raising an eyebrow in my direction, her face sultry, a little insolent. That's a helluva combination.

"Sure, Gillian, but my social calendar's a little busy right now. The murder of Nancy, Blue 27, Bobby gone missing, and, oh, yeah, a certain crime czar named Lenny Cassel, who at one time was hanging out in a certain little hamlet known as the Adora Borealis. And let's not forget two gangsters lying on a slab who tried to kill me and another client, Dawn Stoukas. But, hey, my people will call your people." I winked at her and headed to the door.

One of the buttons on Airedale's double blazer had loosened, opening up the jacket like a bent corner of a paperback. "Cut the comedy, shamus. You're no Soupy Sales."

"I was always partial to Lenny Bruce, bubbie."

Airedale rubbed his hands as if removing chunks of dirt. "Bruce was provocative. He was never funny." He was proud of his pronouncement, a regular Nathan Cohen. "Get out Fuller. Your so-called zingers *bore* me."

"Yours in Blue 27—"

"Get going—"

I spun around and flashed my lopsided lupine grin. "How about Terrien? Either of you seen him around? Ex-hockey player? Small guy? Five foot eight. Hair like a Brillo pad?"

They quit glaring at one another and Airedale took a step back and Gillian's breath quickened. Her shoulders tightened too.

That told me enough.

I pushed back my porkpie. "Where's the tennis racket, paly? You don't look quite at home without it."

He dropped another F-bomb. This time it was an unexploded bomb, lacking conviction.

"We'll do lunch sometime," I said to Gillian.

"Till then." Her face was a fresh sheet of ice, no hairline scratches at all, just clear skin and lips and eyes full of possibilities.

SHE WAS WAITING for me in the car.

Leila. Her breaths were like her voice, coming from a tunnel far away.

Her pale face glowed dimly in the glimmer of the early evening sun splashing red in front of my Ford Galaxie.

"I needed to see you." Her fingers twisted about a large manila envelope.

I tossed my keys onto the dash. "I figured that or you were really into muscle cars." It had a 427 engine.

Leila looked younger without her nurse's cap. Her auburn hair was done in a pageboy cut.

And her eyes were more evenly level than I had thought.

The edges of the manila envelope were worn by the dusty oil of nervous fingers, the clasp in back broken.

I adjusted the car's rearview, and then turned about in the bench seat and looked right at her, my voice low. "You don't need to be scared of me." The inside of my palm still itched a little from the scratch she had served up a few minutes ago.

She wore a light blue jacket over her scrubs. Her red hair was pulled along the tops of her ears with the assist of two tortoise-shell barrettes. Her face was anxious, lips pressed tight, but her eyes were sliding into trusting me.

"And you don't need to be scared about anything else either." I flipped back my blue blazer, flashing my snub-nosed, side-holstered. I had an additional .45 in the glove box. After my tangle with Cassel's goons, Thompson and Langlois, I was packing extra heat.

She nodded, lips loosening into a broken rubber band.

Besides, Leila, I'm parked under a tree, and nobody's around to see us in this car. Toronto wasn't exactly New York. I don't know if you noticed, but this city *does* sleep. We have blue laws. Bits of loose paper and a Styrofoam cup or two kissed the bottom ends of closed-up offices.

But how did she find my car, a '63 Galaxie? Before I could ask, she opened the envelope, the tip of her tongue peeking from a corner of her firm mouth. Her lips were heavy, full. Her nose had a little Bob Hope lift to it. I wondered if she'd had it fixed, like Nancy's. The design looked awfully similar to Nancy's before her face became a Picasso.

Leila slid out an 8x10 photo, black and white. The focus was sharp. Five people on a street, all smiling. The sky behind them black, turning slightly gray from hazy lines of smoke. They stood in front of the Montreal Forum and people ringed about, laughing, hollering, celebrating. There were names written in magic marker under the five principles.

Denys, the one on the far right of the frame, was not looking into the camera, but off to the left. He wore a lambskin hat, black. I couldn't make out any crying fleur-de-lis on his face. Maybe it was on his other cheek, the one not quite visible. He wore jeans and a blazer. He was obviously the self-appointed "artist" of the group, separating himself from the pack, looking in a different direction from their victorious stares. Next to him, a young Bobby Ehle, probably just before his call up to the Leafs, head slightly tossed back with jocularity, comb behind his left ear. Back then, his tan hair wasn't buzzed, it was slicked back, rockabilly style. He wore a white T-shirt and Cuban-heeled boots. Badass. The Beatles before Hamburg. Leaning into Bobby's shoulder, Terry. Also wearing the same get-up as Bobby. He had a comb in his right hand, a big fallen placard in his left, and his pompadour had broken slightly, loose strands twisting across one of his eyes. He looked pouty and sulky, as if he needed a glass of milk before going to bed. A step or two away was Lenny Cassel, the Detroit-area mobster. His hair was charcoal black, his beady eyes pieces of led, and his face stiff, the lips downturned. He was slight, small between the shoulders but he radiated menace. I had no idea that he'd been to Montreal, ever. For five months in 1955, Leila said, Montreal had been his home. Bobby had told her that Lenny was running from a narcotics rap. The last fella, on the far end, lost in a loose-fitting blazer and jeans, a bookend for Denys, was *Guillame*. His hair was buzzed, but it looked like iron filings, prematurely gray or white. His hands were in his pockets. And his face wasn't exactly heavy, but his cheeks sagged and his nose was like mine, somewhat generous. The look on his mismatched face was faraway, not quite radiating the same level of anger as the rest of the posse. *N'oublie jamais* was scrawled above the photo in heavier lines.

N'oublie jamais. Je me souviens. Similar but different. Is this the outfit Bobby was trying to remember? N'oublie jamais.

"Cassel speak French?"

"No." Leila laughed. The photo was taken in the wake of the Richard Riot. "You see the smoke in the background?"

I did. I also saw a line-drawing of a pig and the name Campbell written above it on the placard in Terry's left hand. It pointed down near the ground.

All but two of the participants were smiling: Cassel, the sadistic mobster, and Denys, the artist.

"*Never forget.*" Leila translated the French.

"Yeah, I know."

"You speak French?"

"*Un petit peu.*"

"*Un petit peu.*" She looked away. "That's what this group was against. Second class. French equality."

I nodded. I kind of got the point. I'm a Jew. I know what it means to be an outsider. *Where you from Fuller? You don't look like us. I'm from Toronto, asshole, I was born at St. Mike's. But where you from, your people?*

And then I thought about the fleur-de-lis, the crying one that Denys sported. And then I got to thinking about the half-burned down publishing house in Montreal, and the "bomb" in the newspaper offices of *The Citizen*. It was starting to make sense. Maybe.

"Bobby always said that bilingualism in Canada means being French and having to learn English. It doesn't work the other way around."

"Yeah." It never has worked the other way around. *The English didn't lose at the Plains of Abraham, 1759 or the siege of Montreal, 1760. Conquest of Quebec.*

Bobby was involved in that, the Richard Riot, Leila said. Bobby threw eggs at Clarence S. Campbell. "Campbell was a prick, suspending a French-Canadian hero, and then having the gall to show up at the next Habs game. A real fucking creep."

"Uh-huh." A major fucking creep.

I only wished the creep would let me back in the NHL, revoke my life-time ban.

We're all walking contradictions, I guess.

Leila wasn't at the Richard Riot. She's an Etobicoke girl. But if she were there, she too would have thrown some eggs. Richard was her favorite player. And her father's, even though they were Leaf fans.

Was being a Richard fan a prerequisite for work at Adora

Borealis?

That made her laugh, wrinkles at the corners of her eyes. "No, Mr. Fuller." Her boss admires Richard because he makes you proud to be French.

I could get that.

We all need heroes. *I was always looking for Jewish ones. When I was a kid, my dad went on and on about Barney Ross, the boxer, being one tough Jew. He loved the cat. I too, sought out members of our tribe, cheering for Hank Greenberg in the 1945 World Series. He'd just got back from the War and he kicked ass.*

My father was never my hero.

"You have me at a disadvantage, Leila. I don't know your last name but you know mine. So call me Hayden, huh?" When did women start treating me so formally? I was always Hayden or Hays on the ice. Pretty soon people are going to start calling me hon, like I'm an old man buying postage stamps. Jesus Christ.

Anyway, in 1955, Campbell suspended the Rocket the rest of the regular season and all of the playoffs for attacking an official. Richard would eventually lose the scoring title to teammate Bernie "Boom-Boom" Geoffrion and Montreal would go on to lose the cup to Detroit that spring in seven games. Montreal fans protested, feeling that this was yet another example of English colonial rule. Richard was often viewed as a Christ-like figure by the French media, sacrificing himself game after game, beaten down by the shields and spears of his opponents. They yelled slurs at him: "frog" and "hey, pea soup." I'm proud to say, I never called the Rocket any of that, not once, but I did hit him hard, every chance I got, because, damn it, he was great. Once in a while one of my elbows would ride up a little high, and cut open his face, right under the eyes. I shut him down some games, but more often than not he got the better of me, scoring a goal or two. One night a hat trick. Another night: four goals. Several coaches sent goons over the boards, sticking the Rocket with high crosschecks from behind in every area of the ice.

Not just the corners. He *had* to take matters into his own hands, and during one such after-the-whistle fracas a linesman inadvertently held Richard's arms back allowing Bruin's defenseman Hal Laycoe a clear path to knock Rocket's lights out. Rocket regained his footing, hit the official over the head with his stick, and did a number on Laycoe. Fair-minded people felt the social injustices Richard endured, night after night, but most of English Canada thought Campbell's sentencing was far too light. *Kick him out for a whole season!*

French Canada felt differently.

Bilingualism means being French and having to learn English.

"Denys was the one who threw the canister of tear gas."

"Really?"

That tossed canister forced Montreal to forfeit that night's game against Detroit and Campbell to leave the fabulous Forum under police protection.

Could Denys also send a "tear-gas bomb" to the offices of The Citizen?

Bobby had given this very photo to Leila. The last time he visited. "He wanted me to have it." She looked over her shoulder into the red shadows of the street. "I don't know why." Now Leila wanted me to have it. "I don't know the why of that either." I guess, she didn't think he'd killed Nancy. The drugs made him too tired to do anything.

The Richard Riot, the fleur-de-lis, Denys on the other end of the drug drop gone bad. Did this have anything to do with Expo '67? Airedale's crowd was taking "vague credit," Nancy said for what happened to that literary publishing house.

Leila didn't know. He eyes narrowed.

And who's Guillame? I pointed at the photograph, the little guy with iron filings for hair.

She spoke quickly, her voice still resonating a faint tunnel echo. Guillame had disappeared in the late '50s. He'd be about your age now, Hayden. Maybe a little older. He was a scientist.

Chemistry. There was a car accident. He almost died, and afterward he had enough with science and all, and went onto Copenhagen, Denmark. That was around 1962, Leila said. No, 1963.

She never met Guillame, but Bobby swears he was really strange. Never dated, never interested in girls, or boys for that matter. Maybe boys. At least he was always more comfortable with them. Slight boys. You know, the Nancy boys.

She made a face as if she'd found spiders in her shoes.

"Nancy boys. You mean gay men?"

"Yeah. Anyway, Bobby says Guillame always sat away in the far corners of the booth at the bistros they congregated at. His chair, in the cafes, was the farthest from the table."

"Uh-huh. So he was shy?"

"Chronically. But when he spoke. So much quiet, brutal confidence." She tented her fingertips together and her face was still, following the crawling steps of spiders.

"How so?"

Guillame was the designer of the Richard Riot. He made an impassioned plea at a secret meeting in a dank corner of a Montreal wine cellar and then orchestrated the tear-gas attack. It was all about the birth of a new Quebec, one no longer dominated by old world Catholic values, the Catholic church, and lazy-thinking politicians tied into the conservative hierarchy. It was time for a quiet revolution, a change was a coming. They were no longer going to be the white niggers of Canada.

"Really? He went *there*?"

It was such bullshit. I couldn't say that word, the one that started with N. For me it was the worst word, ever.

"He went more than just there. He wrote-up a whole manifesto: *The White Niggers of Canada.*" It might have even been published she said, by an underground press.

Probably not the press in Montreal that burned half-way down.

"That's how Guillame saw all of French Canada, indentured slaves of the English." Her tented fingers collapsed into a crocheted web.

I nodded again. "So this was the first step in the revolution?"

"I don't know." She looked out the back window of my Galaxie, sighed, and shifted, pushing herself up against the door and its handle. "There hasn't been another step in their revolution in ten years."

I didn't know about that.

Blue 27 could be part of the plan but how?

"Blue 27's a drug that never worked right," she said, her voice falling through a long tunnel.

I disagreed with her about there being no new "steps" in the revolution. A quiet revolution was taking place. Quebec is ready for change. "Pierre Elliot Trudeau's a fast rising French-Canadian star in the Liberal party and he talks quiet revolution rhetoric, moving French Canada out of the shadows of Catholicism and a system of kickbacks and payouts."

Leila liked Trudeau. A lot. "He's sexy."

"So I hear."

Guillame's vision may be more incendiary, but he could still be on the loose. Orchestrating things from Denmark? "I take it he's still there?" *A chemist? What's he mixing up?*

"I guess so." She shrugged. No one in Canada had heard from him in over two years.

"Uh-huh?" Maybe Guillame and Denys were behind the need for those three canisters, the ones Dawn was supposed to deliver to Montreal. *Maybe Bobby broke up that delivery. Why? Could Guillame be plotting a more sinister form of rebellion? A new kind of Blue 27?*

Leila had no idea what I was talking about. All she'd seen of Blue 27 was nothing that would cause any kind of revolution. Dr. Stangl, the chemist working for Airedale and Williams couldn't bake a cake. He was no real doctor, just ex-army, working in radar. What did he really know? Besides, Blue 27 wasn't a weapon—it just slowed you down, made you less inhibited but also took away all initiative. Bobby couldn't even get it up, she said, embarrassed as soon as the words tumbled from her mouth.

"He told you that?"

She looked away. "I'm a nurse. People tell me things."

I wasn't about to tell her about my father.

"Will you testify to this? To the police. About the distribution of illegal drugs—"

"It won't get us anywhere." And it would only get her killed. Again she looked over my bench seat, into the red streets. The sun filled the sky with the luster one expected in Autumn. "I just want to help Bobby." She looked away, eyes misting.

"You're in love with him—"

She nodded. But he wasn't her boyfriend. He didn't even notice her.

I knew a thing or two about that. I reached into the glove box, and pulled out some tissues nestled against my .45. I unfolded the tissues and handed her a couple. "Had Bobby given up?"

I was starting to have my doubts about Oslo, Sweden.

"I don't know if he's given up," Leila said. But she was worried he had. He'd given her one of his Stanley Cup rings.

"Really?"

I'd also have to get Stana looking into Copenhagen, Denmark and the whereabouts of this loose rebel cat, Guillame. I had a feeling he was loose in Montreal. "This Guillame got a last name?"

"Clausen."

"Clausen?"

"It's Danish."

"Danish, huh?" Of course, that's why he fled to Denmark after the auto accident. *Guillame Clausen, chemist.*

"I don't know if Bobby's still alive." Her cheeks were spritzed with light tears. On the last day that she saw him, the last session, on his last dose of Blue 27, falling asleep as he stood up, he handed Leila this photo. "Use it," he said. "I can't."

"Maybe I can," I said. "Maybe I can."

6

Why is it that the people we've made love to and lost, the people we need to move far away from, never ever really leave us? At least for me, a part of myself, my head, my heart, longs to hold onto that younger self that was a part of a life with somebody else. Stana. Her skin still danced with freckles and I remember the feel of her arms, her lips, her hip against mine, the musicality of it all, like drum fills sliding rapidly into a roll, vibrating quickly, her skin pulsing with the blur of two sticks becoming several sticks flashing across a drum head, flash flak rhythms, her rhythms, never the same patterns to her lovemaking, always varying it up like an Art Blakey drum break, her own kind of jazz.

And those eyes, still soldering with commitment to whatever she was working on. And she was *working* on this case. Helping me.

"You're not going to believe what I got for you, today. In fucking credible."

Our relationship was over. The betrayal had ended things, and yet a part of me, the part that resides in the corners of my elbows, the top of my closed eyes, the back of my knees, wanted her. And she looked great this morning, wearing an orange paisley dress with white beads and a black beret slanted to the left. She tapped her chin with the edge of a pencil.

I tried not to let my interest in her show. I looked at the hardwood floors of her office, the nicked-up baseboard, the dusky shoe prints of her colleagues, the lines in the wood. I imagined myself skating between those lines, into pockets of silence.

I wondered if she knew that I was skating to forget her.

"Hayden, focus."

"Sure, sure." I guess she had moved on.

Terry Quinton was back in town.

He had been beaten up pretty badly, but he was okay enough to give a statement. He met the police with a lawyer, a fancy high-brow orator who loved quoting John Donne. Maybe some-day he'll become mayor.

His testimony: Terry flew Bobby up to Vaughan, Ontario, dropped Bobby off at an open field up there. Two cars arrived. One took him away.

A black sedan. A yellow Buick.

"Like out of Dick Tracy color comics?"

"Huh?"

I had been in that car, the last time around, the Stabulas case. Babe Migano. And that was probably his field, the one he was building an amusement park on. Canada's Coney Island in Vaughan, Ontario. *For worms, brave Percy. Fare the well, great heart.*

I too can quote famous writers.

Stana nodded, her pencil no longer tap-tapping.

I wondered how the pickup went down. Did they laugh, smile as they led him to one of the cars or did his shoulders fall, full of resignation and fearful of imminent death? Was Terry Bobby's friend or betrayer?

"His Judas?" Stana leaned forward, seeking clarification.

"Well I'm Jewish. I don't usually go there."

She smiled, freckles dancing in her eyes, pencil tapping, once, twice.

I'd have to see Migano, soon.

Was Migano hiding Bobby or burying him in a field some

place, next to Terrien and Lisa Steinmetz?

Somehow I'm pretty sure Bobby Ehle never got to Oslo, Sweden.

Stana was thinking the same thing.

Anyway, she announced that Terry was back with 590. His story was full of a bunch of nothings. He told the police he thought the early morning flight was all a lark, prep school hijinks, Bobby being Bobby, wanting to be weird, like in his playing days, when he painted the visiting locker room at the Montreal Forum, blue and white, Leafs colors.

"How did he get beat up, then if it's all a bunch of goddamn hijinks?"

"Rolled by a drunk, he said."

"When did he have time to get rolled?"

Stana shrugged, the beret dangling motionlessly. It was a great look for her: arty, liberal, sexy. *Why was she working for a conservative rag like the* Telegram?

"How could Sal let Terry off the hook so—"

"I think he's having him followed, hoping he'll lead us to something bigger. He's playing Terry."

I nodded. "Of course."

Typewriters clacked in the background. Did they ever stop? And the teletype, a slower, less rapid pounding, was ticking away in the left corner. It was 11 a.m., the sun shrouded in clouds, the office a bit dim. Only half of the overhead lights were on.

Terry swore on his rosary beads that he didn't know that Bobby was fleeing a murder rap.

"Uh-huh." I looked at the lights.

Migano also knew Cassel, she said. She had looked into it. Old pals. When Babe was an up and comer in the Montreal gangs, Cassel and he had crossed paths during some drug runs between Montreal and Canada.

"Crossed paths how?"

"Cassel is the godfather for his niece. The one who married

Athol."

"Swell."

I also wondered what went down between them in 1955, the five months Cassel hid out in Montreal. I told Stana about it. Narcotics rap.

Maybe Babe had Cassel holed up in Adora Borealis. I don't think Mr. Machete is still there. I told Stana about my tour of the rooms. *But the room with the pulp novels? I wonder.* Why did Cassel's men try to kill Dawn? "I guess, Dawn's not on Babe's team—" I was thinking out loud.

Stana smiled. "I guess not." She put down her pencil and traced her fingers on her desk blotter around a line drawing of a kite. "Just what do you know about her, about Dawn?"

"What do you mean?"

"Dawn. You seem smitten with her."

"I'm not."

"You like her, I can tell."

"She's twenty-years-old."

"Right."

"I care about her, that's all."

"You care to take a lie detector?"

Jesus Christ. Was Stana jealous? I'd kind of like it if she were. "Dawn was in love with Bobby—I believe that about her. Those tears in my office—"

"Bobby, huh?" Stana paced, the shoulders of her dress tenting slightly every time her pencil missed the blotter and tapped the desk's wood finish. "She's in love with Bobby. Uh-huh." If that's so true, Hayden, why did Nancy never tell me anything about that, huh? I interviewed her. Hours and hours of tapes. She opened a lower desk drawer and pulled out three reel-to-reel tapes. Several of the boxes, with the plaid Scotch brand, were dented in the corners. Rusty tape held lids in place. Nancy said Bobby was depressed, never having got over losing her, that's why he continued to stalk and beat her. He wanted her for himself and no other woman would do. Did he have another woman? If Dawn were that woman, and his alleged girlfriend, why did he not say a word about it to you—

"I don't know. I trust her—"

"You trust too many people."

She looked away. Typewriters clacked. I traced my fingers around the lip of a coffee cup. The ceramic edges were cool.

I topped it off. It was a little sludgy. I made a face.

"I'll make a fresh pot," Stana said.

"Tell me where the stuff is. I'll do it."

She pointed at a corkboard cabinet over a rusty sink.

I poured in the Nescafe and boiled water while talking out loud. So Athol was trying to kill her on Migano's orders because she was betraying Migano? Or Migano, in league with Cassel, was doing the latter crime czar a favor. But what did Dawn have to do with Cassel? She never saw him at the clinic. She saw Terrien, or the presumptive Terrien. Maybe the hit was ordered because Dawn had stolen Cassel's drugs? Migano's drugs? No, the drugs were the exclusive property of The Northern Lights of Beauty. I couldn't figure it. Why the attempted hit?

"Maybe Dawn knew what was in those canisters and stole it for herself. From Bobby, from Adora. And Adora has friends. Cassel." Stana leaned forward, her eyes narrowing. She always had good instincts. "Dawn's trying to make a big score."

"Ransom? Some kind of leverage? I don't know—"

"Dawn never loved Bobby." She returned to the lower desk drawer and threw another manila envelope my way, my second in less than twenty-four hours.

"What about Denys? Who's he in league with?"

"Denys?"

"The guy in the lambskin hat?"

And how did the whole N'oublie jamais crowd fit in, if they did at all?

Stana's eyes were dancing but she wasn't following. "Open the damn envelope. In fucking credible."

"The Richard Riot. The Quiet Revolution?" I waved a hand. "Never mind."

"The envelope—"

Stana lit a Parliament.

I slid out a series of photos: Dawn, lips parted, a man's face buried in her neck, nuzzling her ear, a hand on a left breast, a fleur-de-lis over his left shoulder. Dawn and Terry Quinton, sitting inside Bassel's Restaurant eating hamburgers the size of hubcaps and drinking Molson's, his right hand atop her left wrist, laughing at some event happening outside the frame; Dawn and Terry sitting in his helicopter, awaiting takeoff—she has a clipboard on her lap; Dawn and Terry in Allen Gardens outside the Palm House, a Victorian style building shaped like a Queen's crown, squinting into the sun; Dawn on top of Terry, his bald spot resembling a small, white yarmulke, as her shoulders pull back, her breasts thrust out, and his hands play with her upper arms and a sheet bunches behind her back and nests on top of his lower legs.

"Shit—"

"Does that look like a person in love with Bobby?" The pencil hit blotter, then wood, blotter.

"It looks like I need to talk to Dawn." And Migano. And Terry.

And Bobby. If I ever hear from him. If he's still alive.

"Yeah."

The water boiled. I poured it in the pot, let it percolate.

I pulled down my porkpie and asked Stana to look into a Guillame Clausen. I spelled the name for her. "He was a chemist. Part of the Richard Riot. Wrote a manifesto with a crazy, offensive title." I couldn't repeat those words so I wrote them down for her. "Disappeared around 1963. Copenhagen, Denmark. Check with Interpol, whatever, but find this person."

Her face creased into an abstract painting.

I poured us each a cup of coffee, added one cream and two sugars to hers.

"Maybe check phone records from Adora Borealis." Stangl was no chemist. Guillame was. "Ma Bell might lead us to a contact in Montreal that'll lead us to Guillame." I sipped coffee. The slight burn going down felt good.

She figured she could get the phone records from Sal. She smiled demurely, breathing in the warmth of her cup. "I think he likes me—" She sipped.

"He's married." Two kids, a dog, an above-ground pool.

"I know. I'm just saying—"

"Well, don't say—"

She smiled slightly. Maybe she was getting my drift.

"I think Guillame's in back of this whole thing, somewhere, mixing up Blue 27, planning a possible attack of some kind."

"A hunch?"

"A feeling I have in my gut, and it still feels like shards of dissolving rocks—"

I shuffled through the photos of Dawn. They were done by a professional, the images crisp and clear, the resolution full of deep-focus detail. This person knew how to work expertly with low levels of light.

"Blacks Detective Agency out of Hamilton," Stana said.

"Who hired them?"

They came in the mail. Today. Special delivery from Denise Drouin. Nancy's sister. She had hired Blacks to spy on Bobby, find proof to nail his ass for killing her sister. Their leads led to Terry and from Terry to Dawn and Terry. And from there—

"Denise Drouin, huh?"

Along with the photos, Denise sent a letter long enough to read like a host of UN resolutions, listing her grievances, explaining her motivations. Stana tossed it my way.

It was written by hand. I read it, most of it, quickly. The penmanship was a bit messy, hurried. Denise was a schoolteacher, taking time off to see justice served. She truly believed that Bobby stalked and killed her sister. She was using all of her resources to "bring him down." She repeated that in the letter seven times. I counted.

"Is she legit?" I asked.

I had wondered where Nancy's family was. Usually when someone's brutally murdered family members cry, demand, justice. After her death, not a voice of protest, of sorrow, nothing. Nancy's parents were deceased. Bobby never spoke of a sister, but then again Bobby rarely spoke at all when we suited up for the blue and white.

"I know, right? *Bring him down.* Like she's out of a movie, with her own catch phrase, and not a very good one at that."

"No, no. I was referring to the sister angle. Nancy had a sister?"

Nancy never mentioned her to me, not once, Stana said. All those interviews. No mention of Denise. Stana's pencil tapped out a new rhythm.

"Background checks?"

Stana's lips pushed together. The Department of Motor Vehicles, in Montreal confirmed a registration for one Denise Lucerne Drouin, born October 14, 1933. She also has a registered Social Identification Number and her Birth Certificate checks out. Party affiliation: Liberal. No children. No husband.

"Wow." I sipped more coffee. "Find out what school she teaches at in Quebec. Talk to the Principal. What does he think of her?"

When I was five my school principal thought I was mildly retarded from an early bout with mumps and rubella. I was just chronically shy and didn't talk much back then, but he had sent me to a special school for a week. When I got out, my parents got me a dog.

"You owe me dinner," she said. "And none of those damn street corner hotdogs that you're so fond of."

I like fried chicken, pizza, a hamburger with onion rings.

"We're not talking lo-fi, Hayden."

She was talking like it was a date.

"George's?"

"George's." She agreed.

Maybe she too missed a little of what we once had and both lost. I can dream, can't I?

I'VE NEVER BEEN a big fan of heights. When I was a kid, like four or so, my dad, smelling of Molson's, thought it was real funny to hang me upside down over a balcony at my uncle's place, the one who works construction. It was out in the Scarborough bluffs, and we were fourteen fucking stories up. My uncle and Ma were yelling at my dad to put me down, afraid to rush him, just in case such a choice might startle Pop, so they all laughed nervously, and I just prayed that my feet wouldn't slip out of my Keds. They weren't high tops.

No wonder I was so shy in kindergarten.

Like a dog was going to solve *everything*. Christ.

I never told Dr. Cohen about this episode. Maybe I should, next week.

Anyway, here I was, years later, atop another fourteen or fifteen story building, legs shaking with wind, my porkpie hat threatening to lift off.

Terry Quinton, face full of booze fat, lower lip a small football, was working out some minor kinks and repairs to his 590 CKEY helicopter. He had a wrench or something like it in his left hand and was knocking and pinging about on something down in the nose. My hands were in my pockets, anchoring me in place, at the edges of the landing pad. The high winds puffed open my unbuttoned blazer, flashing glimpses of my side-holstered .38.

I liked the look. It was a good one for me.

I don't think Terry was too impressed. "I don't have to talk

to you, Fuller. You're not po-lice." He came out from inside the
nose and stepped down, joining me on the landing platform.
The air was brisk, the clouds thin ribbons.

I pushed my hand more firmly atop my porkpie, holding it
in place. "No, I'm not the po-lice, but I got the pix, that might
interest the po-lice. Dig? Bedroom pics." I was no beat-genera-
tion cat, but sometimes when I get mad I slip into a voice full of
ersatz jazz.

He pushed his sunglasses against the bridge of his nose. They
were aviator style, and even under the tint lenses his eyes were
puffy.

"You and Dawn."

The wrench quit moving.

And the wind opened my blazer even more.

He moved his feet slowly as he walked a small half-circle.
The landing mat that the copter rested against was gold and the
central design was the Expo '67 logo, a leaf composed of eleven
triangles. At least I think it was a leaf. It looked a little like the
variation on the Star of David. *Right. Star of David. Uh-huh.*

I shrugged, holding the manila envelope, with the six photos,
out toward him. I told him what I knew. He wasn't only involved
with Dawn but also involved in double-crossing Bobby, my client. "You dropped him in a field. That's what the log reports say
and the police report. A field in Vaughan, Ontario. That's land
owned by Migano, the Toronto-area gangster—"

"I don't know no Migano—"

"Right. And I don't know who won the Stanley Cup last year.
Come on." I pointed at him. "Your lips are two footballs and the
sunglasses can't hide the raccoon eyes. Who laid you out and
why? Bobby? Migano?" I wiped the edges of my mouth. "And
don't give me no bullshit about getting rolled by a drunk."

He pushed the glasses further back against the bridge of his
nose and exhaled sharply. "You're still not po-lice."

I held up my hand. "You got me, I'm not." I wanted to erase

his half-circle steps, push him up against the copter's skids, get him to talk. "I guess I better go to the po-lice."

I headed toward the exit door. Green. Thank god it wasn't white and didn't glow. And no one was offering me a glass of goddamn water on the way.

"Wait."

I smiled and loped back to the nose of the helicopter, one hand still on my porkpie. The wind was gusting. "Smart," I said. Look, the police may have believed your story about flying Bobby around on some kind of lark, Bobby being Bobby, but when they see these photos they'll think differently. You had a reason to get rid of him. "You loved his girl."

"Dawn was never Bobby's girl." His eyebrows stretched into a sharp line, a small snake. "They slept together but she was never *his* girl."

"Then why did she tell me she was?"

"I don't know."

I grimaced, my teeth hurting. "What was in the canisters? The ones Dawn delivered that didn't have in them what they were supposed to have in them, the ones Denys was a little angry about?"

"Denys?"

"Yeah. A friend of yours. Richard Riot. 1955. Lambskin hat. Threw a tear-gas bomb. He was on the other end of the so-called drugs-gone-wrong drop. He wasn't too happy."

He might also have tried to burn down a publishing house.

He was surprised I knew about the tear-gas. "I don't know anything about any canisters."

The mention of Denys made him jumpy. His hands twitched at his sides.

"Here's what I think—" I pushed back my porkpie. The wind had died down. Bobby was a courier for Adora. I figured Terry and Dawn pulled a double-cross on Bobby. Took the stuff he was pushing, substituted it with something else, and left him holding the bag, wanted by Migano and Cassel's bunch. "You set him up. And now you've got the bundle, you and Dawn. Whatever the bundle is and are waiting for a payoff."

"That's *your* story."

"A pretty good one too. It's no Maltese Falcon but I give it three out of four smiley faces."

"I loved Bobby. We were like brothers—"

"Yeah. And you led him right to his executioners—"

"I didn't. We were brothers—"

"And now those executioners are going to come for you, the lambskin hat guy. Denys. Your brother."

He said nothing.

"He's got a fleur-de-lis tattoo thing going. Just like you. But why's his crying?"

"Because the French demand justice. N'oublie jamais."

"How come Bobby never got a tattoo?"

"He didn't like needles—scared shitless by them—"

"Of course. So he takes Blue 27 in powder form, right?"

"Yeah."

I had him.

"No, no, Blue 27. What? I know nothing about—"

"It was Blue 27 in the canisters wasn't it? And that's why you stole from him. You and Dawn. A couple of extortionists."

He laughed bitterly. "There's no market for Blue 27. Blue 27 doesn't work." He sat on a workbench covered with flecks of pigeon shit. He rubbed his forehead with a dirty cuff of his coveralls. They were stained with enough oil and grease to heat a subdivision. "It just makes you tired. That's all." He shrugged. Sure, it briefly eliminates pain but it takes away all inhibition and desire. An awkward combination. You feel free to try anything but you have no energy to carry it off. He smiled, his chubby pressed lips resembling a crab's claw. "Nobody wants Blue 27."

"What do they want? Something was supposed to be in those canisters. Something important."

"I know nothing about canisters, okay?"

"What really went down with you and Dawn and Bobby?"

"Nothing." He said something about her being good in bed. The sun reflected off his glasses, filling his eyes with clouded ribbons.

"We had a threesome going. A couple of times. That was it." He smiled. It wasn't pretty. "A ménage a trois, as the French would say."

"Uh-huh." Mr. Culture.

So he really didn't love Dawn either. You don't talk about a girlfriend that way. No wonder he gave her a gold-plated necklace, goddamn four-flusher phony.

I pushed down my porkpie and smiled my lopsided lupine grin.

"So why's the mob trying to kill her? What's the real story? She's not Bobby's girlfriend, she's not yours, apparently. What's the real story?" The edges of my shoulders hurt and my eyes were stinging. Dawn made it seem like it had something to do with Bobby, something to do with the canisters.

"Dawn *thought* I was her boyfriend. So did Bobby. Maybe he knew about us and was setting her up. Ever think of that?"

"Bobby made the switch?"

"Yeah." He looked at his shoes, white sneakers, covered in mud patches of oil. "Yeah. Set her up to get got."

"So Dawn had two boyfriends. Bobby and you?"

"Yeah? Ménage a trois. That's what it means." He looked away and shrugged. "It's 1965. Grow up."

"If that's true, why did he allow you to fly him to safety—if you were in competition for the same girl?"

"It wasn't a competition."

I was confused.

"Besides he never allowed me anything. Allow? He forced me to fly him that night."

So it wasn't a lark.

"He—he—" Terry removed his aviator's glasses. Heavy pouches under his eyes made him squint slightly. The right eye was a series of fish scales. He couldn't see a damn thing out of it and never would again.

"Bobby did that?"

Terry nudged the glasses back in place. "Now, I'm a mechanic. No longer a pilot." His depth perception was all off. He picked up the wrench. "Bobby has a temper, a wicked one. He found out about me and Dawn—"

"I thought it wasn't a competition—"

"Found out about the drugs. Supertuned me. Look, he killed Nancy. No matter how you cut it, he did it."

I exhaled sharply.

Everyone was telling me Bobby did it. I'm funny about things like that. When a narrative gets overdetermined, I distrust the narrative.

"I'm sorry." I didn't know what else to say. "Bobby has the drugs?"

Terry said nothing.

I held onto my porkpie and envisioned pushing my father over the edge.

Blue 27 was created by Guillame Clausen, back in 1959, Terry said.

The chemist, the one that fled to Copenhagen, Denmark?

Terry nodded. He was the guy in the photo with the narrow shoulders and loose-fitting clothes, looking a little lost, or above the fray. He worked for MacMillan Pharmaceuticals in Montreal, seeking out a new kind of Anacin tablet to top all migraines. He started toying around with barbiturate compounds and various anti-psychotics and hallucinogens and discovered Blue 27. The military tried it out with Canada's NATO forces. It didn't work. Sure, it cured pain, temporarily, but it also took away all initiative. Not what our fighting forces want.

Of course not.

1961. Why did Guillame leave Canada?

A car accident.

"That doesn't make people leave their homeland. Come on."

Terry rubbed at one of the hinges of his sunglasses. "Okay, okay, okay." He shielded his eyes from the high sun and said that there was another passenger in the car. It rolled and that passenger, Guillame's lab assistant Gray Davies, wasn't wearing a seatbelt. Dead at the scene. Body mutilated beyond recognition. The car had caught fire. Anyway, Terry snapped his fingers for emphasis. Like that. Done. Here. Gone. Anyway, Guillame didn't report the accident for several hours and the police suspected he was running from a drunk-driving rap. Guillame said he was disoriented after the crash and drifted listlessly about the streets of Montreal, clueless as to who the fuck he was. Amnesia. The foggy forgetfulness eventually cleared and Guillame returned to the scene and called the police. By then the body had been carted away and the gendarmes speculated on pressing charges. An MD testified on Guillame's behalf, saying, after interviewing him, that he believed Guillame's temporary amnesia story. The police, however, were still considering legal proceedings. In the interim, while the gendarmes decided on their next move, Guillame fled to Denmark, telling friends, in a series of postcards, that the sex there was pretty good.

"I heard he wasn't that much into sex. Boys or girls."

"That's true. But Denmark, you know?"

I didn't know.

"Anyway, Guillame's father is Dutch so the kid had dual citizenship."

"Isn't the Dutch thing like the Netherlands?"

"Oh, yeah. Right. His father was Danish."

Next he'll be telling me Guillame made a stopover in Oslo, Sweden.

"You been in contact with Dawn—"

It wasn't a question.

He couldn't look at me.

Of course she'd contact him, police custody or not she'd find a way. She loved him, no matter how much he diminished her in my eyes.

I wanted an address.

He gave it to me.

Nice fella.

Don Mills. Another one of them goddamn high rises. This one a hotel, fourteenth floor. Don Mills and Eglinton.

I handed him the envelope with the photographs. Maybe I should have hung onto them for evidence but it felt like the right thing to do. He smiled meekly.

"Tell me more about N'oublie jamais—"

A bunch of creative young people, artists trying to change the world. Denys was a playwright. Wrote four or five experimental shows performed in Laval. Terry, at one time was a painter in the Renoir mode. Lost interest. Didn't have lasting talent. Bobby was the artist who painted with his skates. Guillame was a scientist, but he was also the brains, the one who wrote up the manifesto, *White Niggers of Canada*, asking for Quebec for Quebecois.

But the title emphasized Canada, so I guess he wasn't a hard-core separatist.

Terry couldn't disagree with that. Guillame did love Canada or the idea of what Canada should be. "You ever notice," Terry pointed a crooked finger, "the street signs in Montreal? They're in French and English."

"Yeah."

"They aren't bilingual in Toronto. Melville, Saskatchewan? English only."

I nodded.

"Being bilingual in Canada means being French having to learn English—"

Bobby had said the exact words to Leila a few days ago, words that must have been memorized as part of the manifesto.

"What about Cassel? He was at the Richard Riot?"

"An interloper. Fleeing some kind of Detroit rap."

"Narcotics?"

"I think he beat up a woman. Broke her nose."

Did he make her look like a Picasso painting? Did he make Nancy look like one?

"So you still in contact with Guillame? Heard anything lately?"

Terry firmly nodded no, his face hard. No postcards, nothing, since summer, 1963. "The same year I quit being interested in hockey." He dropped his hand from the sun.

"1963?"

"The year Montreal traded away Jacques Plante. Broke my heart."

I nodded. "You wouldn't know anyone following me in a silver Chevy Corvair, would ya?" It looked a little gray in the bright sun.

"Can't say I do, 'cause I don't."

Someone was following me. I felt it all afternoon. "Jacques Plante, huh?"

"Greatest goalie ever," Terry said. "The Gumper and Charlie Hodge, forget about it. They're no Jacques Plante."

I guess that would be Terry's answer to the Howe or Richard debate. Jacques Plante, the first goalie to roam from his nets, to wear a mask permanently, to bark orders to his defenseman. The Innovator, the press labeled him.

"This Denys guy, king of the lambskin hat. He got a last name?"

"Denys? Sure he does." He smiled. It filled his face with malice. "But you ain't no po-lice."

7

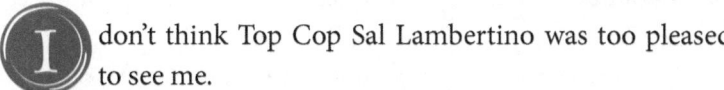don't think Top Cop Sal Lambertino was too pleased to see me.

"What the fuck are you doing here?"

Maybe I should have brought a dozen donuts.

Sal filled the door frame, hands on hips. When Sal was on duty he was a lot bigger than when he was off duty. It was a presence thing.

His mouth worked a piece of gum the size of two jawbreakers.

"Hiya, handsome." I pointed at his puffy lips. "You look like you're hoarding acorns for the winter—"

He shook his head, unimpressed with the wit and wisdom of one Hayden Fuller.

I told him quickly what I heard from Terry about Dawn and Bobby, a threesome, and how Dawn may have lied to us and how I had to talk to her, like right fucking now.

Sweat dotted the top of his forehead, and he quickly looked beyond me into the hallway. He tapped my shoulder and I went in.

Dawn sat on the edge of a couch, hands in her lap, flipped up. She wore dark dress pants and a blue and white middy blouse with crisp shoulders. She looked as if she were about to give a presentation to IBM or christen a ship. When she saw the anger in my face, she spun the bracelet on her right wrist. It became a jet turbine, twisting with enough torque to crash through Mach one. The table was covered with magazines, *Macleans*, *Life*, a small vase crowded with blue dahlias, a *TV Guide*, and a cassette recorder, red with white trim. I noticed because I was so mad I could no longer look directly at her.

The tape recorder wasn't new. A chunk of plastic was missing from a corner and I saw a contact and an edge to one of the batteries.

The tape recorder reminded me of Sal's Ford Falcon with the missing hubcap. With their budget these cops could never eat at Bassels.

"It wasn't Bobby you were in love with but Terry. You work for Terry. You stole from Bobby—for Terry—"

Dawn shifted on the couch, her hands twitching slightly, her clavicles pressing against her middy blouse. The sky in the window behind her was high, bright, cloudless.

"I love them both," she said.

"How did you get this address?" Lambertino side-holstered his weapon. He must've drawn it when I knocked on the door. I hadn't noticed.

"Quinton."

The jawbreaker slid to the other side of Sal's face. He had figured to have Dawn all sewn-up, protected. Twelve or fifteen people came in and out of this room. All police. Part of the detail. All with credentials. Dawn never left the room. She was never alone. The phone was tapped. Jesus Christ.

"Did somebody come clean the room?"

Sal nodded, so did the young woman, thirtyish, sitting across from Dawn. She wore a red-checkered shirt and blue jeans, her hair pulled back severely. Eyebrows lightly penciled and lipstick was drawn from Dawn's fashion élan: 1950s–era bobbysoxer in candy-apple red. None of the lipstick left chipped marks on her teeth.

And her lips were full, like the rooftop of a '49 Mercury.

Officer Sarah Linney was made-up as Dawn, a character in a play. Only I hoped this wasn't a tragedy, because she'd be a hit man's first target.

I gently saluted her with two fingers.

She smiled back, her eyes seizing hold of me, warm, deep dark green, like right after it rains and the sun has yet to return from behind clouds.

"Dawn must have slipped the cleaning lady a note, with a phone number on it, and a ten-spot attached, telling Terry where she is, and Quinton gave up her location. That's the only way it figures."

Sal glared at Dawn. "It figures."

"Twenty," she mumbled.

"And if Quinton gave up Dawn's whereabouts to me he'll certainly give it up to someone else. Someone with more muscle." I punched a fist into an open hand crushing my fingers like cigarettes in an ashtray. "You better move her to another room. Now."

Sal huffed, the fist of gum now on his right side. He dialed the front desk. It was a fast conversation. He snapped the phone back in place. "Give them ten minutes," he said.

I exhaled sharply and told Dawn the truth, as far as Terry tells it. It wasn't Bobby you were in love with but Terry. I got the goddamn surveillance photos from Blacks, a detective agency out of Hamilton who were working for Denise, Nancy's sister.

"I told you. I loved them both."

Right. This is 1965. The so-called permissive society. Go-go dancers and head shops on Yonge Street. Massage parlors. I get it.

The bracelet was now moving counterclockwise.

"Nancy had a sister?"

"She did."

I wondered if the bracelet left a dirty, dingy stain on her wrist? Another *gift* from Terry?

A French song buoyed softly across the room from a porta-
ble Hi-Fi, the music more on the high end, a little tinny, but I
liked the song's folksy strum, and the plaintive lyrics, something
about a girlfriend who doesn't have to be a starlet or wear sunglasses and the speaker loves her and she works at the factory.
Something like that. "Terry's song. Yours and Terry's?"

She nodded. "Jean Ferrat. From France. Terry was big on
him."

"Uh-huh."

Standing in front of the picture window, backlit with blue
denim sky, was a guy in brown: pants, jacket, fedora, with a
white shirt, black tie. He complained about having to hear that
damn fucking song over and over again. Dawn must've had the
stereo's arm set on repeat and this fella was getting queasy from
the three-four beat. He was Sgt. James Moffat, hands deep in his
pockets, reaching, I guessed, for some Rolaids.

"Oh leave her alone," Sarah said. "It relaxes her. Let her relax."

"Right, right." He waved Sarah away with a long-fingered
hand. He and Sarah were partners and both seemed a little tired
of one another.

"It has been over forty plays," Sal said, flat-lining the words.
"Forty."

"Are you going to start in on the kid too?"

"No, Sarah. I'm just saying—"

"Twenty-seven." Sarah's eyes had a slight crease to them.
"Twenty-seven. Soon to be twenty-eight."

The arm circled left, back right, and then hit the vinyl groove
with a carbonated hiss and pop.

I pushed back my porkpie. "Quit spinning the bracelet." It
was hurting my eyes, my head, and I was afraid I was going to
slip into a seizure or something. I still felt a little dizzy from my
mix-up with Lazy Legs. "Why'd you lie to me?"

"I didn't. I said I loved Bobby. I do. But I love Terry more."

"You work for Terry? You stole for Terry, from Bobby."

Lambertino leaned next to my left shoulder, his chunk of gum working its way back over to the other side of his face. It took a lot of effort to get it there.

"We deserve some honest answers. I risked my life for you." I pointed at the officer across from her. "This woman here is risking her life for you—"

"And I believed you too, believed in you." Sal's jawbreaker was trapped under his upper lip, big as a tortoise shell.

The tall angular Moffat, pushed down a crinkle or two on his shirt and moved from the window. He pushed the record button on the cassette player, and gave me the go signal.

"That's why she's wearing your clothes." Sal pointed at Sarah. "She believed in you too."

Dawn looked down, hands twitching like flippers on a pinball machine.

I seized her face and made her look at Sarah, at me, at Sal. "These people are responsible for you, you're responsible to them."

Who knew I was such an existential philosopher.

"It wasn't Bobby who made the switch, but you. You and Terry wanted to make a big score, but Bobby found out, didn't he?"

She nodded again, the light from the window cutting a wide bar across her forehead. She squinted slightly.

Thin ribbons of white were returning to the sky. A stuttering thrush of a helicopter whirred faintly beyond the ribbons. North York General was nearby. Probably a patient being rushed to emergency. There was a pile-up on the Gardiner Expressway. I had heard about it on the radio, on the way over. At least one dead at the scene.

And then there was the silver Corvair, gray in the sun.

"You know anyone in a Corvair, Sal?" I had been followed twice today, a 1964 Corvair. The driver was pretty cagey, keeping three or four cars back, pulling ahead for a while, and then slipping behind. All the way up the Don Valley Parkway to the

Eglinton exit the Corvair moved about like that. The driver had dark hair, sunglasses.

Sal said no idea.

It didn't have a license to go on, but vague dealer plates. I gave him the number. He said he'd check with DMV.

Sal had, however, followed up on Bobby's checkbook. And there were many checks, for big-time dollar amounts, written out to Adora Borealis, big enough amounts to raise some questions about fair-trade practices and have a follow-up interview with Drs. Airedale and Williams.

"Great." I rubbed the edges of my mouth. "You wearing a vest?" I asked officer Linney.

"Yes."

I nodded.

She had been on the force ten years.

I introduced myself.

"I know who you are, Mr. Fuller." A smile spread through her dark green eyes.

I smiled back.

"Game two, 1963 against Detroit you scored the winning goal. Second period, high under the bar."

"Yeah." I scratched a back of a hand against my lips. That was my favorite shot to make, under the bar, tight. "You like this kind of detail?"

"I do my job."

She was a professional.

Dawn said she didn't steal anything from Bobby. She stole from Nancy. Terry knew Bobby and thus had an in at the clinic. And Terry knew Nancy from their Montreal salad days. She was a regular at bistro hangouts in the 1950s when the two attended McGill. Nancy was also at the Richard Riot, throwing eggs, and Terry had slept with her before he met Dawn and knew Nancy was planning on lifting the stuff for "N'oublie jamais," an outfit in Montreal who believed in a free Quebec. She was the one on the train, not Dawn, the one who had to deal with the anger over the double cross.

Why did Dawn tell me she was the one who made the drop? To get my sympathy? Why?

"Did *they* kill her?"

"Maybe." Dawn shrugged. "They were awfully mad." Terry had substituted sugar and baking powder for what Nancy was supposed to deliver and Bobby found out and beat the shit out of Terry, knocking out one of his eyes with his Stanley Cup ring. The one he wears on his left hand. And then he took the goods with him.

He didn't have the ring on his left hand when he visited with me in my bungalow three days ago. I wonder if that was the one he gave Leila.

And no wonder Terry struggled to keep the over-sized dragonfly above the horizon line that first night at my place, he was flying with one eye.

"Bobby took the goods. To sell on the open market?"

Dawn didn't know.

"Did he do it to protect Nancy, to protect her from committing a treasonous act?"

She didn't know about that either.

I don't think Dawn would make a strong *Jeopardy* contestant. She didn't know shit.

"So nobody was ever trying to kill you—"

"No." She fought back an urge to cry, gasping without opening her mouth. The threat of death, that part of the story was true. She did see Athol stalking her, after the bad drop.

"Athol wanted you dead?"

"Yes."

So Bobby was in league with Migano?

Athol also had a connection with Cassel. The Detroit area mobster and master of the machete was the godfather to Athol's wife or something or other. I'd have to re-check my notes.

"When Terry made the switch who was he going to leverage the drugs with? Was it Migano? Or Cassel?"

More shit she didn't know. All she knew was a pair of heists took place: Terry and Dawn from Nancy; Bobby from Terry and Dawn.

All for blue 27? It was a goddamn drug that didn't even work. At least not that well "I don't buy it, Dawn." My face slipped out of my lopsided lupine grin. "What was supposed to be in the canisters that Nancy was delivering to N'oublie jamais?"

She looked at the floor. A small patch of carpet was covered with bits of candy wrappers that resembled giant chunks of popcorn.

She had been eating assorted truffles.

"Who are these Never Forget people?" Sal tossed his chunk of gum into a nearby trash bin. It thudded, a heavy meteorite.

"I know nothing about N'oublie jamais," Dawn said.

Nancy knew something, some vague credit the Airedale clinic was taking for a half-burned out publishing house.

"Not sure who they are," I said. They wrote a manifesto, one Guillame Classen wrote it. Find him. He's supposed to be in Denmark. "I think he's here. In Canada. Most likely Montreal. He helped organize the Richard Riot."

I filled Sal in on the photograph with the Campbell placard and how three of the five players (Bobby, Denys, Terry) from the then Richard Riot were all present and accounted for in this caper. Two from the infamous photograph: Guillame, the little guy with the large nose and iron filings for hair, and Cassel, a modern-day Houdini, were somewhat less accounted for. Was Cassel ever at Airedale's? Nancy said she saw him there and then Nancy got got.

Dawn wiped her hands on the sides of her hips, and pushed up from the couch, moving to the Hi-Fi. Apparently, she was tired of the song. I hoped that maybe it suggested that she was tired of Terry too. The way Terry talked about Dawn and Bobby and him, the sideways nasty smile, the self-satisfied leer, the disparaging underbelly to all he said, made him an unrepentant toad. He and his threesomes.

"I'll get it," Officer Linney offered. "What do you want to hear?"

"Sinatra. Ballads. Anything sad." Dawn sank into the cushy center pillow of the couch. The lines in her blouse crisp, freshly pressed.

"I haven't forgotten my original question. What was in the canisters, Dawn?"

"I don't know."

"I don't believe you—"

She couldn't look at me. Detective Moffat rubbed at his stubble, filing it down with the edge of a heavy hand, and then a distant whir-whir cluttered the room, like my rattling fan with the loose ball bearing, hammering a thousand timpani's together, and then a short burst, followed by a longer burst and triangles of glass splintering the room, and a dotted checkered shirt, falling, and I pushed Dawn from the couch, banging the side of my face on the coffee table, and the room became louder, whirring, spinning with ten thousand timpani's. A hundred thousand. A million.

I looked up.

Officer Linney, eyes filmy, her body torn, lay on her side, face to face with me, and Sal crouched low, hands gripping his gun, firing out the window. The helicopter dipped and then rose, and hovered left and away.

Sal kept firing through broken glass.

He reloaded.

Wind rustled the room.

Sal didn't stop until his gun was empty.

WE WERE IN A DIFFERENT room. This one had less windows and smelled of cigarettes and cleanser. It was blue, from the curtains to the carpet. Even the cedar trim that covered half the walls was blue in the dim light.

Minutes ago they had taken Sarah Linney out in a body bag.

The bullet-proof vest wasn't enough.

"I wish I could've thrown you out that broken window, bitch." Moffat raised a tired arm and then dropped it, his voice sinking with the gesture. "That was my partner, you got killed." Tears filled his voice. He pinched at his eyes. "My partner. Do you hear me? My partner."

Nobody said a thing.

Terry Quinton was also dead. Sal had just got the call from HQ that Quinton was found on top of CKEY's office building, his throat slit wide, and "N'oublie jamais" scrawled with his blood all over the Expo '67 logo. The helicopter was gone. Who flew it? And who fired the rounds of machine gun bursts? Two different people.

And neither of the two was Terry Quinton. The MD said that rigor mortis indicated he had been dead too long to have been doing much of anything during the timeframe of the attack on Linney, who was supposed to be Dawn.

My money was on the guy with the lambskin hat and crying fleur-de-lis tattoo. Denys with no last name.

Dawn was spread across the bed, on top of the covers, her legs on the floor, her arms folded on her chest. Tears crowded her eyes.

One of the medics wanted to give her a sedative but Sal waved him and his damn suggestion away. He wanted answers. Now.

Moffat was mumbling on about Sarah, her husband, two kids. He said something about ten years. His left hand trembled as he wiped at the filed-down stubble and hardened blood on his chin. I think one of his fingers was broken. It dangled at an acute angle.

Dawn stared at the lines in the ceiling, locking on the hexagonal shaped light fixture, and the broken off pieces of flies and bugs netting the fixture's center with shallow ashes. "I didn't want this to happen to her." Her voice was nearly an inaudible whisper. "She was a good person."

"She was," I said.

"Goddamn window. I should have pushed you out of it." Moffat was full of sulky languor. "I still might."

"That'll be enough," I said. "Enough. Who left the goddamn drapes wide open?"

Nobody said a thing.

"Fucking bitch." Moffat again, leaning, lifting a bent, tired arm that resembled a broken curtain.

"Did you hear me?"

He took a step or two back, his eyes lean, unmoving, his hands hanging at his sides still trembling. His chin was full of pepperoni blood.

I sat next to Dawn on the bed, touching her face, pushing wet hair from eyes. "I'm sorry about, Terry. I really am."

Tears slipped away.

I still cared about that girl I gave twenty dollars too, the girl whose mother had disavowed any connection to following her involvement with dangerous men and sex parties, the girl who liked to listen to Jean Ferrat, the girl who, like the singer praises, doesn't need sunglasses or a movie star's face to be beautiful.

"He doesn't quite say that." She laughed. Her wet matted hair resembled discarded pick up sticks. I wanted to kiss her, tell her that she was loved.

"I need your help, Dawn. Please."

Sgt. Moffat, his hat twirling in his right hand, reluctantly moved toward the coffee table and punched on the tape recorder. The back of his hand was raw from where he scraped it on some broken glass.

"You better get that finger set," I said.

He shrugged.

"Dawn what really went wrong with the drop?" I wanted her

theory. I didn't care if it was totally right, what do you really think happened, no bullshit. I smiled a watered-down version of my lopsided grin and removed another tendril of hair from her face.

She smiled awkwardly, teeth touching.

I kissed her nose.

Nancy did do the drop. That's for sure, Dawn said. That's what happened. Dawn wanted nothing to do with it all. At first. But Terry kept asking her. It was like he needed her to do this, to prove her love for him. He kept pushing that idea, how much do you love me, really, and so she did it, switching out the drugs with sugar and baking powder. The original drugs were in small red packets that looked like those condom packages you'd pick up at a lonely out of the way gas station. One of those vending things you slide a dime in? You know, in the men's room?

"Red? Red packages."

"Yes."

"Not Blue 27."

"No."

"Something else?"

"Probably."

"How many of these packages were in each canister?" Sal huffed, his face unreadable, eyes heavy.

"Two, three hundred."

Sal let out a low, sharp whistle.

Adora Borealis was behind the manufacture and pushing of the drugs. They cooked them up in a lab at the clinic, but not in the lab I had seen, that, with its pristine blue cabinets and scrubbed white tiled floors, was a dummy for the public. "There's another lab," she said.

"Where?"

Next to the hydrotherapy room. Between the second and main floor. "You know with the mirrored glass?"

"Yeah?"

"There's a lab under that." A section of the building had a dropped floor or a half floor like the stacks in university libraries. That part of the building wasn't two stories but two and a half.

"A hidden floor?"

Yes, she said. And you had to keep your head low. The girls were okay, but the fellas were always having to duck, to keep from bumping up against the ceiling.

"Girls? How many working in the lab?"

Seven or so, Dawn said, and they were all naked, covered with spots of powder, little constellations, as they mixed up and cut the drugs and put them in the red packages. It was Airdale's idea to have all the girls naked. It prevented individual pilfering. "That's what he called it. Individual pilfering. A total ass—"

"A pompous ass—" Him and his quoting of John Donne.

"But I suspect he just liked looking at our titties." She smiled weakly. She said our. I didn't miss that.

Dawn squinted at the ceiling, as if counting each ash in the light fixture.

"I thought you worked at Eaton's, the toy department?"

"That's what I tell people."

Dawn, lab worker. For a couple of months, anyway, while working on her GED. It was good money, and Terry, one of Airedale's couriers, flying junk up to northern Ontario, was always there, kibbutzing with her, saying he liked her eyes, while looking at the spots of powder on her tits and navel, and they had a good laugh about that, and then he asked her out, and that's when she found out all about Nancy, and Terry's scheme to double-cross her. Bobby was at the lab a lot, too, picking up his fixes of Blue 27, and patting Dawn on the fanny, saying how good it was seeing her naked again, and this time without a fez on her head. It was funny what he could remember because he had forgotten so much, but the fez, that he remembered. At first it was just staring and teasing, but Bobby eventually opened up about being Bobby. "I guess I have one of those faces that people want to share things with." She shrugged. He shared about his headaches, his pain, his problems with his ex, his inability to sustain an erection, and how Blue 27 was a temporary fix, relieving pain but taking away his ambition. "One day, he kissed me. And then he did it again. And then Terry saw and suggested he join us. In bed."

"Uh-huh."

It didn't go well. The threesome.

"Bobby pushed up against me, my hip, touched me, kissed, me, but he couldn't get hard, and he watched Terry and I finish up, and then Bobby cried. For twenty minutes." Terry had tried to console him, but the bawling Bobby punched Terry in the solar plexus, winding him, leaving the room. Two days later Terry wanted to get back at Bobby and Nancy and make a big score. She wiped the tears at the corner of her eyes. "But there was something we never counted on."

"What's that?"

"The merchandise had changed." They were no longer pushing Blue 27. The red packages weren't like the blues at all. The reds were crammed with something new, much more dangerous. Her eyes zeroed in on the light fixture. "We didn't know what it was—"

"A new drug?"

"Alex Stangl discovered it—"

"I doubt it," I said. "That guy couldn't find his car in a small parking lot. Guillame was a chemist. He's back here. He's working on this shit."

Dawn knew no Guillame.

Sal wanted to know more about the new drug.

It wasn't a pain reliever, Dawn said. The opposite actually. It was made to inflict pain, but that's all she knew.

"Was Bobby in on this new drug? Was he on it?" I wondered if he used it to kill Nancy.

"I don't know."

I rubbed Dawn's left shoulder. It was tight, full of sand. I rubbed harder. "Could he be?"

"Maybe."

Dawn had no idea.

Bobby may have been the test case. They got him to take the drug. He killed his wife and then they, whoever they all are, knew it worked wonders.

Maybe whoever killed Terry and Sarah was also on this junk. Could it be Bobby?

"Is Airedale the top man? Is he the one in charge of this racket?" Sal's jaw jutted forward and his eyes were locked tight. "Or is it Williams?"

Dawn only saw Airedale, he was the one always there in the lab, getting a good look at the naked girls, copping a feel now and then for laughs, always touching. "We girls called him Dr. Cops a Feel. That's why I wanted to steal the shit, when I thought it was Blue 27, to get even with him. But if I knew—"

"Is Williams involved in trafficking?"

"Yes." Well, she then said, she wasn't 100% sure. Eight-five per cent. Dawn rolled sideways and then on her back, arms straight at her side as if she were standing at attention while lying in bed.

"You never saw her in the lab?"

She didn't. But how could she not know, Dawn wondered. She shared the office with Baggy Ass.

And Gillian Williams wasn't carrying his tennis rackets. She was a smart woman.

And then I thought about Cassel and the day I got to check the rooms there, the room with the pulp paperbacks and Pepto-Bismol. Was Cassel whisked away, hiding out in the half-floor of the lab? Nancy had seen Cassel there. My feeling was that he was still there. Why hadn't he left? That was the bigger question.

"So, if Bobby took the drugs from you and Terry, what did Bobby do with them and where are they now?" Sal placed a hand on top of the television. He drummed an erratic pattern, rushing tempo. Maybe he should have taken up the saxophone.

"A bigger question," I offered, "How much more of this new drug are they going to produce?"

"We'll get that stopped," Sal promised. He got on the phone and called the judge in our last case, the one who's a Habs fan.

"Migano," I said. "Bobby took the stuff to Migano."

"We're green lit." Sal smacked the phone back in place. "We'll have the warrant soon." He paced and let out a slow breath that was a skinny skip of air. He picked up the phone. It was time to call the Linney family.

Dawn returned to counting ashes.

8

It didn't surprise me at all that we didn't find a damn thing at Adora Borealis. There had to be a leak somewhere, someone who was always tipping off Airedale and Williams, making us a step late, slow. I'm not a paranoid person, but this case had me convinced that the bad guys had moles, television monitors, and wire taps everywhere. Maybe I ought to check in with Dr. Cohen.

Anyway, we had our warrant, yellow police tape, X's, everywhere, and all the rooms, except for the woman who nods, were empty. The hardboiled paperbacks were still in room seven, but it appeared unoccupied and Cassel was a no-show. What struck me odd about room seven this time were the switch plates, four of them, low on each wall. They weren't outlets, but more like a path for sending a signal, like a closed circuit TV signal.

The lab? It was low-ceilinged, but not a drop of powder blue or any drug-related evidence: balancing scales, beakers, nothing. Instead, the cramped room, which felt like a crumpling cave, was full of uneven shelves, old *How and Why Wonder Books*, turpentine and paint cans, white of course. During the course of our explorations, Dr. Cliff Airedale repeatedly raised his fists and shouted how we were infringing upon his civil liberties. He wore a different colored blazer but it had the same crown on the left breast pocket.

Sal kept banging his head on the low ceiling and letting out 57 varieties of expletives.

Cliff drank water, a lot of water. Stopping at every alcove. The water was so clear as to not be water. There were no blemishes, no bubbles, nothing. It was mercury in a thermometer without the red tinting.

I still wanted to hand him a damn tennis racket.

Dr. Gillian Williams, her face impassive, lips pinched, also drank a lot of water, while floating two steps behind Police Chief Sal Lambertino, who was rubbing his noggin. She tilted her head left while showcasing the hydrotherapy room and its seven tubs and their nozzles and foam guns. She even let us in on the room behind the mirrors. It featured a long, narrow conference table, punctuated by seven or eight phones, and ashtrays for everyone. A blackboard ran along the opposite wall and was full of ideas for marketing their new projected products, including "Jouissance," a female lubricant. I guess Stangl really was working on that.

Jouissance. I kid you not.

Off to the left of the command office's conference table and fleet of phones was a pale green door, not white, but this door had an equally big handle like you'd find on a submarine hatch, that led to the half floor and rags and paint and paper towels and cleaning supplies. A waste of space, a total phony, that half floor room. Something much more important had to have been going on there. What was tossed in appeared hurried and it showed. *The How and Why Wonder Books* was the tip-off. Those were for grade school kids. And the cans of paint: ten years old.

They wanted to make it look like an unused junk room, an elaborate closet, but I wasn't buying. Maybe they should have thrown in a beat up trap set and broken-stringed guitar for the convincer.

Gillian smiled a lot, sipping water during our "tour," leaving one-third empty glasses everywhere, nodding quickly, answering questions. And she moved like she had taken ballet lessons: shoulders back, head up, feet balanced. Barbara Stanwyck in *Double Indemnity*.

Once or twice she made a point of nudging next to me. She was no longer in my back pocket, but there were agendas behind her body touching mine. The first time she apologized; the second time she smiled; the third time, breasts against my chest and arm, her lips parted.

What about the checks Bobby had written for such astronomical amounts? Sal cited some of the totals and Gillian looked at Airedale who was still citing a list of civil liberties being breeched and she said, I guess it's okay to tell you, Cliff won't mind, but Bobby was a regular who believed in our product and was buying into the business. Those checks signified down payments to join their team. Bobby was going to be one of their partners. She could send the police the paperwork in a few days if they wish. Sal wished.

"This new drug, in red packages? Was that part of the business Bobby was buying a piece of?" Sometimes Sal lacks all nuance.

"I don't know what you mean."

Sal twirled his hat in his hands, lips pressed tight. "I think you do—"

Airedale raised his fist again, prattling on about the police persecution.

"Lenny Cassel, the gangster. Nancy saw him here."

"Well, Nancy's dead. God rest her soul. Perhaps she suffered from some form of hysteria. Lord knows she had hang-ups." She smiled in the direction of Airedale, then at me, her teeth perfect.

I wondered if she knew about my hang-ups?

Everything about Gillian was too, too perfect, from her petite-balanced figure to her delicate nose and wideset, soulful eyes. The only thing off, the hair. The platinum glow looked a little too green in Adora Borealis's track lighting, like she'd been swimming too long in chlorine.

But it was the smile, slight, full of a whimsical distance, a Mona Lisa Smile. Sexy, arty, and unintentionally intimidating.

It kind of got to me and kept me away simultaneously.

"Terry, one of your associates, we understand, ran drugs—"

"If you got that information from Dawn, who can trust her?" Airedale smiled.

His face wasn't full of whimsical distance. Instead, there was a bit of a sneer to his smile and I wanted to knock his teeth out and then kick him in the face for mumbling.

"We know she posed nude for art photos," he said, imagining the sessions taking place before him, now.

That was my last case. The one involving Maple Leaf Gardens. And Dawn was hypnotized when she did the posing.

She wasn't responsible for posing nude, asshole.

Stana posed nude for art photos too. Private ones. A free choice of love. Just for me. 1962–63.

"That girl, Dawn, even had a fez on her head. No clothes, just the fez. I wouldn't trust any testimony from such a character. Wait til my lawyers—"

How did he know about the fez?

Did Bobby tell him?

Did Airedale run with the Coughlins crowd, a secret gentleman's club that was part of my last case?

"You better get some lawyers, pal," I said. "What about Denys? Lambskin hat?"

"Who? I thought the hipsters went out with the Beats in the '50s." He laughed. It was a little tinny. "With that get-up, this fella Denys could play the fool in modern-day version of Lear."

"Oh, so you did read a book once, huh?"

That pissed him off, his eyes filling with anger. "Your quips are very droll, Mr. Fuller."

"Get those lawyers ready, asshole. We're going to keep an eye on this place," Sal promised, pointing his hat as if it were a stiff Billy club. I guess there was still a little blue in all that Sloan Wilson gray. "Who comes in, who goes out."

"That's harassment," Airedale shouted.

"That's police work," Sal said.

I'm not quite sure that came out right. Anyway.

"Let's go," Sal said.

His team followed him out the main doors of the lobby. A couple of fingerprint men remained, dusting. I didn't expect they'd find much of anything.

On my way out, Gillian's shoulder nudged up against mine for the fourth time, and she put a little more breast into it. She whispered, "Dinner tonight?"

I paused, pulled down my porkpie. I was supposed to go to George's with Stana.

She gave me her slight, Mona Lisa smile, whimsical, playful.

"Cassel *was* here," she said. "But that's off the record." She drank from a fresh glass of water. "I need to talk."

"So, he's not here, now?"

"No. *Cassel* isn't."

I was wondering if she was wanting to broker some kind of deal. "Tonight then—"

"Where?"

She smelled great. Northern pine trees. "George's?"

I felt like a heel for suggesting such a thing.

"George's," she said, her nipples pushing through the bra she wore, pressing against the fabric of her blouse.

"George's," I repeated, my affirmation full of wandering steps.

THE CEILING WAS HIGH, vaulted. The fire place, a stone circle, topped with books, briefcases, and newspapers. Babe Migano's upscale home in Etobicoke resembled a ski lodge and I wondered where I should park my boots and poles.

"Can't you get some new material?" groaned Athol Leighton, the bowler plunked tightly on his head.

I forgot I made that joke last time I was here.

"Jesus Christ." He shook his head, his left hand inside his sport coat. He grimaced. Athol reminded me of Napoleon with indigestion.

"Bad escargots?" This was a "French" case so I was being relevant, making with the French-flavored zingers.

He shook his head and belched.

"Linguine, definitely linguine, heavy on the alfredo. Can I recommend the salad next time?"

"Shut the fuck up. Wait here."

He lumbered to the room at the end of a long hall, his shoulders pushing him forward, a hand still inside his sport coat.

A huge cedar door, the size of two, opened, and Babe Migano with a raised eyebrow nod, crossed the room, his face freshly shaved, a red rose in the lapel of his pinstripe suit. "Hayden Fuller, the boy with the chutzpah. Mazeltov, my Jewish friend."

"Thanks for agreeing to see me, Babe."

"Nonsense." He smiled, took me by the arm and led me to his office, a low-lit room, full of rare first editions and a faint haze of blue cigar smoke. A glass taboret stacked with fine bourbon and three shot glasses was by the side of his oak-top desk. A series of photographs of people having fun at Coney Island, circa 1920s, was on the wall behind him. Cheap Amusements. I pointed at the photographs. I wish I too were falling from the sky on thin wires like those of the parachute ride.

"I stare at them all day long," Babe said, acknowledging my stare. Sometimes he wished he could be a kid again and then he wouldn't have to deal with all the messes that come with being a restauranteur.

"What about other messes?"

"Such as?"

I sat across from him. My chair was kind of big and made me look small. His chair was a little smaller and made the big man look even bigger. On several fingers were rings.

"Drugs that come in red packages?"

He had heard of them. He looked at his fingers. "Three missing canisters—"

I was taken aback by his directness. "You don't have them?"

Of course. People talk. He didn't know where they were, but he knew of them. And if he did know where, he wouldn't sell them on the open market, ever, that's for sure. The jag-offs pushing this stuff weren't patriots. This was a new Canada and he was in on the party. The libre Quebec crowd could kiss his Dago ass. They were messing with his livelihood.

He waved Athol away.

A hand, inside his blazer, Athol belched quietly on his way out.

"Salad, buddy, keep pushing the salad."

"Shut up, Fuller."

"How do you feel about Expo?" Babe leaned forward and poured himself a glass of Blanton's bourbon. He poured me a seltzer and dipped in a wedge of lemon.

I didn't think about it one way or the other. "It's okay." In 1967, Canada would be 100 years young, and the city of Montreal was hosting the World's Fair. The Expo exhibit was labeled "Man and his World" and Canada had been awarded the bid in 1962 after the Soviets backed out. In 1967, the Soviets would be celebrating fifty glorious years of communism.

Irony intended.

"Some people don't like it. Some of Airedale's crowd," Babe said.

"What do you mean?"

"Nancy hinted to Bobby and Bobby acted—quickly and with extreme prejudice."

"She tell him about vague hints and the publishing house fire?"

"That and other things. The detractors of Expo hated the whole show. They feel the city of Montreal didn't have the real-estate to host such an event. Damn, they needed 64 city blocks. So what does Mayor Drapeau do? He builds the habitat right on the St. Lawrence River. Brilliant."

It was. Drapeau and his team created an amuse-ment-park island. It figures Babe would love that. So far 25 million tons of silt had been dumped into the St. Lawrence to build the land mass. Twenty-five million. Some think they'll need fifteen million more to touch-up the project.

"But some parts of French Canada, Hayden, aren't too big on celebrating what feels like another example of En-glish colonialism."

The Conquest of Quebec, 1760.

He leaned back in his chair, smiling. "They think the money can be spent on better things: education, infra-structure, making Canada more French."

"Uh-huh."

"So they got themselves a weapon. Red 45."

"Red 45?"

"The drugs in the canisters. That's the street name." Bobby had told him all this.

"You've seen Bobby?"

"Of course."

"And he's still alive?"

"Please. Don't make me sensitive." He knocked back a finger of bourbon. Poured another glass. It was a dark amber gold, burned honey. "Of course he's still alive." He smiled. "I'm a business man." Another smile. "Most of the time."

"What kind of weapon and who are they?"

Kids from the old neighborhood, disgruntled. They weren't able to figure out the Canadian dream. He knocked back his second shot. He knew them all, operated a candy shop on St. Catherine's Street years ago and some of these kids ran small errands for him, collecting for the numbers racket. Bobby was just ten then. Harmless, cared about the community, shoveled sidewalks for his neighbors, made some extra money to put food on his mother's table. Bobby didn't have a father. Terry. He was a little shit even then. Never shoveled sidewalks and didn't always return all the cash he received, a regular goniff. "You like the Yid word, Fuller? I'm speaking your language, paisan. Anyway, Terry would short me, nickels, dimes and I'd have to smack him around a little. Capiche?"

I nodded. "Bobby brought you the—"

"No. He didn't bring me the canisters. He hid them somewhere—"

"So you're holding him prisoner to find out where this junk is?"

"Would I do that?" He pulled out a small plastic container from his pocket and spritzed the rose in his lapel. "You're making me sensitive again."

Right, you're a business man.

"I can *hear* you. You're thinking out loud, Fuller."

"Sorry."

I do that. With all the concussions I suffered as a hockey player I often find my censor's checked out, playing golf somewhere.

Bobby's a patriot, Babe said. He cared about the kid. He was giving him refuge until this whole thing blows over and the truth comes out.

"What if the truth comes out not in his favor?"

"Then I'll send him somewhere."

"Sweden?"

"Somewhere." Look, Babe said, Bobby may have run with those Quiet Revolution folks, but he was a federalist, a union guy. "Of course this is all off the record, shamus. You understand?"

I sipped my seltzer. "What do these people want? How are drugs going to hurt Expo '67?"

"Want? I'm not even sure they know. Really. They think they're bringing France to Canada. The people of France don't really even like us. They think we're too undignified for them, lacking in clear, plain-speaking argot. We're the bastards of their republic."

"I thought de Gaulle's behind the Quebecois."

"Anything for a headline. de Gaulle. Please." Look at the mess he made with Algiers.

I forgot that Babe, by association, felt he was part French. He had lived in Montreal for years.

Those canisters contained anywhere from 600-900 packets of Red 45, I figured. "If you have them, you should turn it over to the authorities."

"I don't." He reiterated how Bobby had hid them some-place. Babe opened the drawer to his desk, and jacketed a round into the chamber of his .45. He dropped it on the desk blotter. "I'm going to take down Airedale. That fuck's gotta get got."

"He's behind all this?"

"That's why I got this." He pointed at the piece. "They, this crowd, want to mess up the party, Expo '67." And Red 45 was a hell of a shit disturber. It acts on anger. It makes people want to kill without being aware of what they did. Like Blue 27 it has a forgetting component, amnesia, but it moves people beyond their consciences, outside of judgment.

I exhaled sharply. No remorse, no regrets.

Could Bobby have been a test case? Could they have got him to kill Nancy?

"How are these people going to use Red 45 to start a revolution?"

"Well let's call it a diversion, shall we?" He took another sip. "Revolution? Not likely. Diversion, yes. You heard about the 'bomb' at *The Citizen*?"

"Yeah."

"Chump change. Their idea, it seems, is to drug Mayor Drapeau with this shit and other followers of the old Duplesis regime, Members of Parliament. Mess up the House of Commons. A variation on Guy Fawkes day."

"Uh-huh."

"And then. This makes more sense." Babe smiled. It was a little bit wobbly. "Get the powders, Red 45, and spread the stuff through water."

I whistled. "Fuck."

He poured a third shot. "Uh-huh."

"Water filtration plants. Fuck up a lot of people. Divert attention, pull focus from Expo."

People killing people. Indiscriminately. That's what this drug allegedly makes you do, Babe said. If you have a deep-seated hate, that part of the brain triggered for anger, your oxytocin receptors, get overstimulated to the point you act out that anger, hate.

I said nothing. I'm no scientist, but I got the gist. *Flash Gordon Conquers Expo.*

The hands on the small clock of his desk stuttered. "Who's Denys, Denys something or other? Got a crying fleur-de-lis on his face."

"Denys Goyette, the Brain, they call him. Not much of a brain really. I mean who the hell puts a tattoo on their face?"

"What about Guillame?"

"The fairy?"

"The chemist."

"He's in Holland, isn't he?"

"Denmark."

"No idea."

"I think he's here and behind all this."

"Could be." He knocked back the shot. "What do you want from me?"

"Leave Dawn alone."

He laughed. "Dawn?"

"Dawn Stoukas."

"Yeah, I know who Dawn Stoukas is. The chick in the fez."

"Yes, the chick in the fez. Leave her alone."

"I didn't know I was pursuing her. I'm practically a married man." He smiled.

"Call off Athol."

Babe's face turned to crumpled-up paper. "What about Athol?"

"He followed Dawn with intentional malice all through the R.O.M the other day."

"Those weren't my orders."

"Whose orders was he following then?"

Babe's eyes narrowed. He opened the desk drawer again, took out a small wedge of paper and wrote a note and scrawled his name. He handed it to me. "My marker. It's a gambling term."

"I know what it is—"

I'd seen *Guys and Dolls*.

"You never go to the track. You never drink. What do you do for fun?"

"When I'm working I'm working," I said. I liked donuts, bowling a few frames, and any film with Paul Newman. That guy is badass.

"That's my marker, my I.O.U., my promise not to hurt Dawn." He held up his hand as if preparing to take the witness stand.

I pocketed the note. "Cassel's no longer at Adora?"

"I don't know anything about Cassel either."

"Isn't he your pal?"

Babe made a jerking off gesture.

"Something about a nephew or a niece—?"

"Cassel's got no hold over me. I hate his punk ass."

Christ, I guess times had changed, niece or no niece.

"Bobby?"

"He's alive." He adjusted the cufflinks poking from the arms of his pinstripe jacket and snapped his fingers. Athol returned, rolling in a cart with a huge machine on the lower shelf. The machine looked like a mini Hi-Fi. It was a videocassette recorder, Babe said, three-quarter inch tape, the kind used by CBC to archive hockey games. They film the games right off the TV screen with 16mm cameras and then store the material on videotape.

I wondered how he got his hands on such advanced technology.

"A guy lost a lot of money in a poker game at White Heat," Babe's high-end restaurant. He smiled. He nodded sideways at Athol and Athol slid a tape, the size of a porter-house steak, into the machine. Snow appeared and then an image: Bobby from high above, sitting upright in a chair, coiled rubber tubing around his chest, wires flowing from a few fingers. He was taking a polygraph. I recognized the guy administering it. He worked at the Bay Street police station.

Babe had connections.

The questions were straight forward and simple. What's your favorite color, what was the name of your first dog, did you kill your wife?

It looked, by the cedar trim, and high ceiling, like it was filmed in Migano's living room. At one moment, when the camera pulled out for a wider shot, I thought I saw a corner of the stone circled fireplace.

And my ski poles.

Question after question. The tape ran for twenty, maybe thirty minutes. Bobby passed with flying colors. There were very few blips on the polygraph paper. Only one: did you hate your wife? "No?" Bobby answered the question with a question. When asked again, he said no with a more robust tone and the lines spiked. But when asked if he killed her and answered no, the graph didn't spike.

The expert held up the scores for the camera, and said that, in his opinion Bobby Ehle truly believes he didn't kill Nancy Drouin.

However, he did hate his wife. For the record, the expert said. Full disclosure.

"A polygraph doesn't mean much, Babe." Let's face it, I said. Red 45 makes you forget. So does Blue 27. Maybe he just doesn't remember and truly believes he didn't do it but *truly did*. Maybe, in time, he will believe he did it.

"Maybe." Babe lit a cigar. "Maybe." But Babe believed him. He knew Bobby as a kid. He was a gentle person.

Bobby insisted on the lie detector. "He did it for you. He wanted you to believe in him." Babe shrugged nonchalantly.

"Sure—" But all those concussions, the years of marital discord, the abuse of Blue 27? What if Stana's right? Bobby's fourth face denies the actions of the third, refusing to acknowledge its violent history. I'd seen the photographs. Nancy's disfigured face. I told Babe about those photographs, that history.

"Nancy was a good woman, a good-looking woman. Bobby shouldn't have done what he did. Never hit a woman." He played with a bulky ring on a pinky. "But he didn't kill her—"

Athol was looking away at the golf-ball like dimples on his Florsheims.

"What if Bobby's memory returns and he discovers—I mean, what if—"

"If that happens—" Babe looked into his empty glass of bourbon, twirling in his right hand. "If that happens, Bobby couldn't live with that kind of truth."

"The final taxi?"

The glass stopped twirling. "Huh?"

"A suicide, a hearse, a funeral."

"Right." He laughed. "Final taxi. I like that. It's the one ride we don't have to pay the fare."

"So how long can you keep him locked in a candy store?"

Babe smiled. He wasn't sure, but he cared about Bobby, and he wanted to keep him safe. He was there at Bobby's confirmation, his first hockey game, his wedding.

"And you're trying to get his cache of Red 45?"

"I'm a businessman, Hayden. I don't deal in that kind of business." He believed in putting Canada first. This was a young country, a great country. "Bobby's protecting all of us from ourselves by hiding it."

A patriot, huh?

"You wouldn't have someone in a silver Corvair, looks kind of gray in the sun, following me, would you?"

"I wouldn't drive a car like that or let any of my friends behind the wheel. They don't handle well. They're not safe."

I guess, he'd test-driven a few.

"How are things with Kim?" Kim Stabulas, one of the girls in my last case.

"She's the girl I'm going to marry." Babe hadn't posted the banns yet because all the troubles with Bobby had him preoccupied.

"I don't know if you can protect him, Babe." I thought Bobby should come forward, turn himself in, get medical help, psychiatric help.

"A head shrinker?"

"Yeah." I think, if he killed Nancy, the extenuating circumstances will set him free.

Extenuating circumstances would not give Bobby his freedom but a death sentence. So for now, he feels like he didn't do it. "Let's keep it that way."

"Is he really heading to Oslo, Sweden?"

"Oslo, Sweden?"

"Inside joke."

"I can't say where he's heading but he's heading somewhere." And it was neither Norway or Sweden, Babe assured me.

"You really love Bobby."

"Was there ever any doubt?" Babe smiled. His flower seemed to be smiling too.

9

Gillian Williams looked awful good. She wore cream-colored slacks and a blouse with a brown sweater vest. Her shoes were two-toned—tan brown with white looking doilies for the inlets and laces. Her purse was brown. Her lipstick and nail polish cream-colored. She knew how to accessorize.

Me, I wore a blue suit, a powder-blue shirt, a new tie, and left my porkpie at home.

It was my gentlemanly look, de-accessorizing.

We sat at a back table, a red and white checkered cloth giving our space at George's an added intimacy. Gillian had escargots with her meal. I noshed on Italian bread with garlic butter.

A candle, with a strong angular flame, burned yellow between us.

And I felt guilty as hell. I was supposed to have taken Stana here, tonight. Instead I was sitting across from Gillian, staring into gentle candle flames.

And she looked awful good.

"So what's on your mind?" I folded my arms on my chest, leaned back.

She pursed her lips tight, in a French way, and smiled whimsically. Cassel was on her mind. Her blue expansive eyes glanced around the restaurant, taking in strangers,

quickly darting about for anyone who may be an enemy.
I guess pushing drugs can do that to you. I wasn't quite
sure how deep her involvement in trafficking Blue 27 and
working alongside Cliff Airdale went.

But I was sure of one thing. She was no ingénue.

And that certainty led to a second one: be careful, this
might be a setup.

I stole furtive glances at her beauty—the fine line of
her cameo-style neck, her delicate cheekbones, pencil thin
eyebrows, full sassy hair—afraid of having my look captured and contained by her.

She peeked over a left shoulder, right. The 1950s were all
about bust lines, hips, and curves. She was 1960s beautiful.

She sloughed an escargot from its shell.

It wasn't done with malice but a gentle, quiet gesture. If
I weren't stealing looks I wouldn't have noticed.

Worm for sale.

Kids on a softball diamond down by the Humber River.
The sun bleeding across a low horizon line. I'm eleven or
twelve, pounding a fist in my mitt, listening to them poking fun at French Canadians and their struggles with English, dropping the "s" in plural constructions, worm for
worms. Big joke. Worm for sale.

*How do you think your accent would sound to them if
you tried to speak French, dickhead?*

Me, I don't have an accent, Fuller, they'd say.

I couldn't stop talking about it. Worm for sale. Instead of peeking over shoulders, I was peeking over my
past, apologizing to her and all of French Canada for the
sense of social injustice that occurred daily throughout my
childhood.

"Am I trying to too hard to tell you I'm not like those
other kids on the softball diamond?" I admired the French,
what they had to put up with, all the English businesses in

Quebec hiring their own over French people, and I have a soft spot for chocolate croissants.

"Your love for French culture makes me think I might have a chance with you."

I didn't look away fast enough. I was caught in her eyes. "I, uh—"

She liked the vulnerability in me. My eyes lived there, in that space, she said.

I smiled. What would Dr. Cohen have to say about that, huh? *Vulnerability, Dr. C, vulnerability. That's what Gillian said. I swear it.*

Be on your guard Fuller. Could be a setup.

"So much pain—"

"I get by." I watched the candle's flame stretching taller.

She smiled, teeth perfect. "Doug Harvey, huh? You really think he's the greatest?"

"Yeah."

Richard for her, was the ambassador for French Canada, no doubt. She too was there at the infamous Richard Riot. "Over the years the amount of people at the Forum that night has grown to a quarter of a million. But I really was there."

With Cassel.

"Come again?" Cassel was an American but his mother's family was French and he'd often visit Montreal. "Isn't that Tim Horton over there?"

It was. All the Leafs came to George's Spaghetti House on Dundas and Sherbourne. It's not far from the Gardens. It was their hangout, away from Hugh "Two Fisted" Farrell and his streetcars.

"What were you going to say about Cassel?" Was he the person in the Corvair tracking me, watching me? The Corvair's dealer plates were a phony according to Sal. The car was never registered.

Cassel was at Adora Borealis. And still is.

I stopped pushing a twirl of spaghetti against my spoon. "What?"

She slid a key in my direction. It was green, a Yale brand, with a gray putty smudge on its top edge. It nudged under the rim of my plate and stayed there. "Room 7."

But don't call the police, please. She didn't trust them. There had to be a mole. On the police force. If I brought Lambertino and his men over, Cassel would surely disappear.

And she'd be dead.

"That sounds like high-blown melodrama," I said. "How would you be dead?"

"Trust me." Her eyes held mine, filling me with her detached whimsicality.

I couldn't possibly understand how Cassel could still be hiding there. We knew all about the half-floor and we searched and searched—

"The mole gave us plenty of time to re-locate him."

"Uh-huh."

She wanted to broker a deal. She'd give up Cassel if I'd agree to put in a good word on her behalf with the police. Her involvement in this case was extenuating. If the police barge in, her life could be in jeopardy. She wiped gently at the corners of the mouth. She was tired of it all. Room seven. The one with the pulp novels and cabinet full of over-the-counter relief for indigestion.

"What's Airedale got on you?"

"It's not him. It's Cassel."

"What's he got?"

Gillian knew Lenny in Montreal back in 1954–56. Cassel played in the AHL with the Providence Reds. Won the Calder Cup in 1955. He was a decent two-way forward, feisty, but never got the call-up to the NHL. Anyway, because of his French-Canadian Mom, he often visited the area in the off-season, sometimes during the season. He knew the whole gang: Denys, Gillian, Terry. "Palled around with us all."

"Uh-huh."

"His best friend was Guillame."

"The chemist?"

She nodded. Some people thought Cassel was a little funny on Guillame, had a thing for him. Kind of a crush. She looked toward the back exit, the front door. Her fork gently tapped her plate with a trace note or two. "Cassel was taken with him." Her face was an immobile portrait. "In love—"

"I see."

"I never liked Cassel much. Too brash. Typical American. Loud."

I nodded.

"But he knows me." She rolled spaghetti against her spoon. Her lips pinched together into a pouty French-shaped circle. "And when the troubles in Detroit started—"

"Troubles? He hacked two people to death with a machete—"

"When that mess hit the proverbial fan he came to me for help. Pulled on our prior friendship."

"Blackmail—"

"No, no a favor."

"A favor? You mean blackmail."

She ate her crushed circle of spaghetti. Her wide-set eyes glinted.

So she agreed to help him because of a connection the two forged over ten years ago. Airedale, being the asshole that he is, insisted that Cassel earn his keep, $50,000. Cassel obliged.

I let out a low whistle. "That's a lot of keep."

"Airedale's a bastard."

"You don't like him much."

Her porcelain face remained impassive. Only her eyes moved, revealing the glare she felt toward him. "No," she whispered. "No." She touched up her lipstick. "No."

That was one more "no" than I expected. She really did hate him. "So, why the change of heart? Why come to me?" I couldn't figure this. She does a favor and now she was turning Cassel over. And I wasn't sure about the no police part of the equation either. Something smelled like a big fat phony and I wasn't about to be a patsy.

She pushed aside her spoon and fork. We'd both lost our appetites. "Nobody knows this." Her chin dropped slightly, her lipstick glistened. There wasn't a blemish on her face. "Nobody knows this, nobody." Her fingers tented together. "They'll have no record of her disappearance."

I knew someone else like that. Dead and no one knows. Brian "Spinner" Terrien, buried in a field.

"Leila. She's dead."

Leila, the woman with the heavy face and autumnal hair, the one I promised to protect.

"She found out who he really was—"

Was there ever any doubt? He was front-page headlines on every paper from here to Montreal.

"We did some work on his face. Airedale and I." Slight, she said, but enough to make him a new person.

"A fourth face," I mumbled like Brando. That's the only language, besides English that I speak fluently. Marlon Brando.

"A fourth face?"

"A theory." I explained it, how Stana had christened it. I talked some more about what a good reporter she was, but I didn't confess to how Stana's not being here made the back of my neck and shoulder blades tingle with guilt.

Nor did I confess to how catching glimmers of Gillian through angular light made the guilt even worse. I'll have to send Stana fifty flowers to make this right. Maybe even a new pair of pumps, Maple Leaf blue. She always looked good in blue.

So Cassel could now board a plane to Sweden. He and his fourth face. "And let me guess, coach hockey?"

Her lips parted and the lines around the top of her eyes appeared slightly downturned. "Yes, how'd you know?"

"What does Bobby have to do with all this? He was going to coach hockey in Sweden too."

"That's right," she said. The plan was for Bobby to get plastic surgery while over there. And then join Cassel as fresh talent from Canada. Of course they'd change their names to some obscure forgotten players. AHL types that no one remembers.

"So how did Cassel kill her. Leila?"

I'm not sure why I needed to know, but I did.

"His hands." Gillian wiped at her mouth with the back of a small hand. She grimaced, her chin wrinkling, the lines forming into an upside-down horseshoe. "I liked her." She looked at her discarded spoon, spots of dark marinara hardening in its center.

"Me too."

"Oh, you had a conversation with her?"

"Un petit peu."

Another smile. After the killing, which was so pointless, Gillian had enough with harboring such a sociopath. Cassel didn't have to kill Leila. He enjoyed the excuse that allowed him to do so. As he strangled her, Cassel claimed he counted the seconds, seven, it took for her to die. It was just a game to him, a crazy game. A cheap amusement.

"And I don't quite get your game." I pointed a fork at her. "Why can't the police just go in and bust his ass?" Take some guns, take him out.

The leak, the mole. I told you. The mole. In the police department. Inside. That mole would tell Cliff and he'd figure me for the traitor, she said. Cassel would get hid and after the police found nothing Cassel would add one more victim to his killing floor. "With me, he'd probably use the machete."

"Why's the fuck still holed up in your place?"

They were waiting for the plastic surgery to heal and he was almost set to leave, but after he killed Leila and she scratched his face with her hands, they had to do some touch-ups. It would be a few more days before he'd leave Canada with a fourth face.

"Who's the leak?"

Gillian didn't know. If she did, she'd tell me. It was someone on Lambertino's staff that's all she could figure.

Sarah Linney's death at the high-rise hotel took place in a room full of five people: Lambertino, Linney, Moffat, Stoukas and me. Five of us. Who left the goddamn drapes open? What did I know about Sgt. Moffat? Of course, there were a lot of other people on that particular detail who came in and out of the room. Twelve-to-fifteen, Sal said. When the shots were fired, however, it was just us five.

And the drapes were open. Wide.

Christ. I wish I would've thought to have closed them.

Gillian shook her head. She knew no Moffat.

Neither of us could touch our food. Rocks were dissolving in my stomach. Gillian, as always, was composed, her face a calm lake.

There are a lot of other people on Sal's staff, people I didn't know. Any one of them could be Airedale's go-to.

And what about the person following me in the Corvair? Silver, gray in the sun? Could that be our mole?

I couldn't see Cassel driving a Corvair. Too much ego. A

Cadillac. Black, she said.

I sipped seltzer water, Gillian pale beer. The tan color matched her purse and shoes. Even what she drank fit her accessories. Tomorrow I'd send ten shares of Nestlé's chocolates to Stana. Make it up to her somehow. Bassel's? I might even drink a Guinness with her.

Gillian pulled out a compact, powdered a spot on her chin. "If it wasn't for this case and me being on the other side, I could go for you."

I can't sleep with someone unless I love them. Old school. Squaresville.

"But wouldn't it be fun to mess around?" This was the 1960s. It wasn't our mothers' time, Hayden. Join the permissive society.

She reached for and touched my hand, fingers full of fire. "We could make love, once, no strings. I would never tell anyone about it—"

The words were wrong, forbidden words, a secret kind of love.

"I value my freedom too much to—" She shrugged in the middle of her pitch.

"What time tonight do you want me to fish out Mr. Machete?"

Just after two a.m. The nurses switch shifts then. I could sneak in during the interim.

"Airedale won't be there?"

"You kidding? The guy has banker hours. Ten a.m. to 3 p.m."

She was still holding my hand. I motioned for the check. "Back to my earlier question." I pressed my hands together. "What does Cassel have on you?"

"What do you mean?"

"To do such a favor." Harbor a fugitive, perform minor plastic surgery, help get him into Sweden. Shit like that.

"This isn't about friendship. You don't even like this socio-pathic cat."

No, she didn't like him. Much. Anymore. It was about Guillame Clausen. "My best friend." Cassel, at one time, was crazy over Guillame. "If I didn't help Cassel, he was going to expose Guillame as the chemist, the mastermind behind Red 45."

"The plot to poison the water filtration plants around Montreal and pull focus from Expo?"

Gillian was surprised over what all I knew.

Did she know that I knew that Bobby had 600-900 pack-ets of that shit hid somewhere?

Cassel and Gillian, back in the mid-1950s went to beat poetry readings and shared a passion for French politics and the burgeoning need for a quiet revolution. "I was smitten. But he never could see me."

"Cassel knows where Guillame is?"

"Yes."

"Where?"

"Close by."

"Montreal?"

"A suburb there. In Montreal. That's their base of oper-ation."

"Look, you got to go to the police. You give them this in-formation, they'll give you a goddamn medal. All charges will be dropped."

She couldn't do that. She cared too much about Guil-lame.

The waitress in a black turtleneck and slacks returned with the check and a phone with a long chord on some kind of gold platter. She placed them on the table. "For you, Miss Williams." She handed her the receiver.

Gillian smiled absently. For the first time her sexy whimsicality had become awkward, every gesture losing its sharp focus.

Tentatively she spoke into the phone. "Yes—thank, you—" She turned sideways in her chair, one leg over the other, the phone caught like an errant Frisbee, between shoulder and ear. "No, I don't think so. No. I can't—yes—a guest—"

I tried focusing on the candle, but I couldn't help overhearing. It was my job to eavesdrop.

"That's not a good idea. You need—no—Guillame, listen—"

Guillame. The voice bleeding out of the dial was slightly elevated with a nervous, adenoidal whisper.

I leaned forward in my chair, huffed sharply, the candle between us puffing once or twice, and then it continued burning a longer flame.

"We'll talk later. I don't think—Guillame—listen—no—later—"

She held out the dead receiver.

"Long distance?" I heard her start the conversation by accepting the charges. "Collect?"

"Yes—Montreal." She couldn't look at me.

It was him, she confessed, eyes on her hands, still holding the dead phone. Guillame wanted to put his plan into action, now, yesterday, the day before yesterday. He was impatient, and she was trying to talk him down. He was a troubled person.

"The plan? The water filtration plan?"

"Yes."

He often called for advice, particularly when he was in a manic phase or a terrible blue mood, as he called it. "He's a genius, but moody. Very moody." She looked through my shoulder.

"Moody enough to unleash Red 45?"

She nodded. "I told you he was a troubled person." Her

calm face was the very cup of trembling. There was no absolution possible for Guillame and possibly for all of us, she said.

"What about all the troubled persons who'll drink water tainted with Red 45?"

She was aware of that. It took a subtle approach when talking to Guillame. Always subtle.

"How did he know you were here?"

"They have ways." Her blue eyes had lost some of their stillness.

"They?"

"They. N'oublie jamais."

"Is Denys, Lambskin Hat, part of this outfit?"

"I don't like him—"

"You've seen him?"

"He knows Cliff." She held up two fingers curling together. "Tight."

"How big's the organization?"

"I'm being followed. Constantly." She figured maybe the Corvair was a part of their outfit.

She pushed her hands together, played with the collar on her blouse, adjusted the lines in her sweater vest. Her goal was to keep Guillame calm, work on his better side, reach his conscience.

I wondered if Sal had those phone records yet from Adora Borealis. They surely should lead right to Dr. Frankenstein. In Montreal.

"You got to turn him in. It's your duty."

"I'll turn in Cassel. To you. And we'll see where that leads." With time Guillame would soften. "The way he talked now. Manic phase. He's always talking extremes when in that stage, but he'll come out of it, soon." She was sure of it. Her face losing its calm trembling.

Soften? What if Bobby's not the great patriot Babe makes

him out to be and has plans to return Red 45 to Guillame, or, even worse sell it on the open market? How much more of that junk could be cooked up by Guillame and shipped onto the streets of Laval and Montreal?

"Do you know why Guillame went to Copenhagen, Denmark?"

"Sure. Relatives." The seltzer was too warm.

The waitress retrieved the phone with the long cord and I handed her my Diner's card.

The call was long distance. When it comes in, charge me, I said. She nodded and left.

Relatives? In Denmark? No, Hayden, that wasn't it. Gillian took in a deep breath and ice cubes clacked in her water glass. The water here was nowhere near as good as the filtered stuff at Adora Borealis, she said. But she drank some anyway. The cubes noisy chipped marbles as she parked the glass to the side of her plate.

Guillame, according to Gillian, wasn't happy in his own skin, in trying to be a man. His hands were too small, his feet dainty, the distance between his shoulders slight. Yes, he had a man's nose, a rather generous one like yours, Hayden, but Guillame always felt like a woman trapped in a man's body. Denmark is one of the leading places in the world for sex reassignment surgery. That's why Guillame went there. Not to be with relatives, not to escape the gendarmes, but to be re-made, re-modeled. He was placed on the reassignment list, underwent psychological evaluation, even had his nose adjusted, thinned, but in the end couldn't do it. Instead of being re-made he remained. A man with a new nose, a more feminine nose, but still a man.

"Wow." I was Brando again, inarticulately looking down at my plate, the spaghetti drying.

Cassel loved Guillame, but not as a man. He wanted the sex change. It's complicated, Gillian said, because Guillame wanted it too, and openly shared this with Lenny, his desire to become a woman, even taking on early hormone treatments, but as the surgery loomed, he had doubts, and those doubts got more desperate as Guillame feared losing his relationship with Cassel. He wrote several long letters to Gillian explaining his confusion, his desire to be both sexes, but he ultimately decided to remain what he was born with: a Nancy-boy fella who was constantly teased and ridiculed for not being manly enough.

"And your loyalty to Guillame is such you feel a need to protect him and thus were willing to go along with Cassel's demands?"

"Yes."

"To coach hockey. In Sweden."

"Yes."

It sounded so ludicrous. A Detroit-area mobster, a machete wielding czar, turned hockey instructor and coach. "I'm telling you, turn this info over to Sal's team and they'll give you a medal."

"I can't. I think I'm in love with Guillame too."

"I see."

She smiled, her lips a thin wave. Guillame is a very mixed-up man, unsure of his identity in a rapidly changing world. "I mean some men are now growing their hair out, looking like women."

My smile joined hers. I still sported a buzz cut.

She shrugged, one shoulder rising higher than the other. "I had to help him."

"Of course."

I pocketed the key. Room seven. Two o-five a.m.

"I'll leave the light on," she said, and then winked.

I WASN'T TOO PLEASED when I got back to my bungalow in the suburbs. Someone had tossed the joint. The mattress was ripped off the bed and slit down the middle; the pillows on the couch were gashed with a serrated knife, chunks of foam spilling out of jagged slits like dropped intestines. Jazz records, abandoned and tossed, slipped from their sleeves and were discarded akimbo hubcaps. My filing cabinet was upended and loose-leaf papers ran across the dining table and over the top of jazz records. Plates and glasses were broken in the kitchen.

And to think, I was planning to sit down and read for a couple of hours.

Mickey Spillane. *The Girl Hunters.*

What were they looking for?

Stana's topless photos from 1962–63 were still there. In a manila envelope. The clasp broken.

I didn't know if I should be offended that they hadn't taken them. They were low-key noir images, shot with an ISO of 100, a 1/200 shutter speed, the F stop set at 1.4. I was proud of the work. Stana was beautiful.

She still is.

Shit. I placed the photos back in a lower desk drawer and cleaned and oiled my gun, re-aligning the firing pin. Then I loaded it, snapped shut the chamber, and dropped an extra six shells in the pocket of my windbreaker.

I scrubbed my hands clean with Comet, and turned to the fridge and made myself a quick Swiss pastrami sandwich on rye with mayo and a side of kosher dill pickles. Glass of orange juice.

I hadn't eaten well in a few days. The spaghetti dinner at George's just didn't sit well. I was supposed to have been there with Stana.

I got ready to call her when my phone jarred loudly.

Gillian.

"Hey, what's up?" I already felt I'd spent too much time with her. I wanted to talk to Stana.

"Well, that doesn't sound too friendly—" Her words purred like a Peugot.

I switched the phone to my left ear. "Sorry. I had just sat down to a bite—"

"George's wasn't very appetizing?"

"I was tense the whole time—and I can't eat when I'm tense." There's a lot of things I can't do when I'm tense.

"I know what can help you unwind—" The purr to her voice had popped into a higher rev.

"I'm too tired—I'll—"

"Raincheck?"

"Maybe."

There was a long silence, the phone's static light snowfall.

"I want to rest up before—"

"I can be a great sleeping pill." The purr was Mona Lisa whimsy.

"Do you have any idea who might have broken into my home—rifled my files—"

"It was broken into?"

"While we were dining at George's." *Coincidence?* "Come on. Don't bullshit me. Did you set me up?"

"No." Static snow swirled between us. "I tried telling you they were watching us. They knew—"

"I got to go. My sandwich is getting cold." I like pastrami cold.

"That's not the only thing that's cold right now." The purr of her voice had become grinding gears.

"I'm sorry. I—"

"Good luck tonight."

She kissed the receiver.

It smacked my ear.

I wasn't sure if she were being ironic.

I ate half the sandwich and called Stana. Her voice was

distracted. I wondered if she had company, a fella.

"I call at a bad time?" What business is it of mine if she were on a date?

"No, no." She had just nodded off watching TV. "What is it?"

I told her about my conversation with Gillian, not the latest one, the one at George's, and the part about Guillame and Copenhagen and the possible sex change operation. He got his nose fixed, but that's about it. "Can you look into it? Fact check?"

She could.

There was also a Corvair that was following me.

Yes. Silver. Looks kind of gray in the sun? Apparently, it was following her too. This afternoon, as she left the *Tely*'s Front Street office, the Corvair tagged behind her to a local A&P where Stana bought an apple and some brie. She hadn't been eating too well lately either.

I promised to make it up to her. Bassel's in a day or two?"

She wanted George's.

I didn't dare confess that that's where I took Gillian.

I also didn't confess to Stana Gillian's human sleeping pills pitch.

I did tell her about Denys. Gillian's slim connection, how she didn't like him much. A paint thinner glaze of hate coated her eyes when she spoke briefly of him.

Oh, Stana said. "Yeah. That guy. The one in the lambskin hat, Denys Goyette?" He's not just a former playwright but a hit man, she said. Two newspaper informants, an ex-mobster turned politician and an associate of Migano's who insisted on anonymity, knew of at least four hits in the last six months claimed by Goyette.

"Who's he work for?"

"Freelance." Her voice parachuted to a whisper. "Goyette was probably the gunman in the helicopter."

"That makes six," I said. "Six kills in six months." Terry and Sarah.

"Yes," she said, all of her words falling slowly. "No doubt he's mixed up with that Red 45 crowd. Guillame hired him."

"Yeah." Guillame. I wondered what he looked like now.

"Probably heavier with a thinner nose," she said.

Did Denys kill Nancy?

"Not his style. He doesn't use his hands." Stana was still convinced that that murder was Bobby's.

"Look, if you don't hear from me by noon tomorrow—"

"What?"

"Never mind."

"You can tell me, Hayden." Her words were no longer softly falling.

I guess I wanted to tell her or else I wouldn't have called in the first place. Two a.m., I had a key, Adora, going to get Cassel.

"He's there?"

"Yes."

"Don't do it alone."

Like me, she thought this might be a setup. Stana didn't buy Gillian's rationale for a covert op. "Bullshit, bullshit, bullshit" was all she had to say on that subject.

"I love you," I said, my voice now dropping like a parachute. I was afraid she didn't feel the same. "I just wanted you to know in case—"

Static gently buzz-buzzed between us.

"You hear what I said, Hayden? Don't go in alone."

"I got my friends, Smith and Wesson."

"Don't be a smart-ass." She figured this setup for a real phony, better call Sal.

So I did.

WE SYNCHRONIZED our watches. My Galaxie was parked on a deserted side street from Adora. A trash dumpster was to our left and the black alley was charred black logs. 1:46 a.m.

I gripped a smudged key in my left hand. It was supposed to unlock a back door. I toyed with the tacky substance atop the key, by the Yale name.

"What about the room, room seven?"

I didn't have a key for that.

"Christ, Fuller." Sal shook his head and rubbed at the traces of his Hemingway beard. "Details aren't your bag—"

I laughed. "No. I guess not."

"Shit. Details. I didn't bring my badge."

We didn't have a warrant so he wasn't a cop anymore. Just a fellow citizen, helping a friend.

I nodded, grateful for his company.

Unlike Stana, Sal figured there was some truth to Gillian's yarn. If he brought in a full platoon of cops, word would get out and we'd be playing button-button with Cassel. There most definitely was a leak and it was under his watch and that pissed him off. After Linney's death, he wasn't sure who he could trust.

"Who opened the curtains in Dawn's room, the day Sarah got shot?" I pushed back my porkpie. It was good to have it on again. I felt naked at George's.

Sal had no idea. Like he said before, twelve to fifteen personnel went through that room. Could have been anyone. Could have been Dawn herself. "But I doubt it."

"What if Dawn wasn't the target?"

"I don't follow?"

"What if Sarah were the target all along?" I pulled on the brim of my porkpie. "We're getting tripped up because she was wearing Dawn's clothes, but what if the killer knew that?"

Sal pushed himself back in the bench seat and the color of his face turned to ashes.

"What was she working on?"

"The Stoukas detail." He shuffled a Rothman's from his deck of smokes. Lit it. "The other day I saw her talking to some high ranking officials, upstairs, behind a frosted glass door—"

"Internal Affairs?"

"Looked like RCMP."

He asked Officer Linney about it later and she said it was a cold-case file they were following up on, something about the Marilyn Cozart case, the sixteen-year-old girl who disappeared from Toronto four years ago and was last seen in a lakefront bar in Buffalo.

What if she were blowing smoke, Sal, and it was this case, this one right now?

Sal nodded, taking a long, slow drag.

I suggested that when we get done with Cassel that we go through all of Linney's files, everything, all the cases she was working up.

"Yes. Let's." He took another drag and tossed his cigarette through the open window. It arced and sparked when it bounced along the pavement.

I checked my side-holstered weapon. My hand shook. "I appreciate you being in on this with me, Sal. It means a lot to me."

"You need a hug or something? I got Lifesavers."

That cracked me. "Let's go."

The alley's shadows were full of Neolithic monsters and splashes of conical light. We darted through the darkness.

THE HALLS OF ADORA, with its faint red runners glinting instead of the bright fire of the overhead track lighting, looked narrower. We wore PF Flyers, giving us quiet stealth. Quickly we moved through the hall to the L part of the building, the wing away from the hydrotherapy unit and the drop floor. A central-air system, pumping coolant, hummed off and on.

I couldn't control my breathing. It kept catching and I felt as if I were about to drown.

Around the elbow of the L, voices, women. One nurse was replacing the other. The accent of the older woman was crisp, clear, bright leaves on an autumn afternoon. The other voice was faint, lost in the rumble of a subway tunnel.

Leila.

She wasn't dead.

I'm pretty sure that was her voice, beyond the building's elbow. Leila.

I jotted a quick note and handed it to Sal.

He couldn't figure what the fuck the scrawl meant.

I neglected to fill him in on the alleged murder of Leila at the hands of one Lenny Cassel, machete-wielding sociopath. I didn't tell Stana about it either. Sometimes my head works as slow as Bobby's.

Sal jotted on the back of the note: abort the mission? *We being set up?*

Probably. But we didn't have time to get out of here quick enough without being detected. What the fuck, let's get Cassel and shut this place down.

A dark line was at the bottom of the door to room seven. I grabbed my flashlight, my gun was in my other hand.

A faint cigar smell bled from under the door.

It wasn't fresh.

And the voices beyond the elbow. Moving. Our way.

Sal nodded, motioned toward the door handle, nodded "no," locked, then he held up two fingers. He was going in first. I was to follow.

His right foot bashed the door back.

Arc light flashed the room, the shelves, pulp paperbacks, an ashtray, two crushed cigars, on a nightstand, a face.

Tight curly hair, like a Brillo pad. Eyes closely set. The space between his shoulders, slight.

Terrien. Brian "Spinner" Terrien, the man I saw die, an eye hanging from its orbital bone, his last breath, bubble-gum blood.

"Hello, Hayden. Taken any good photos lately?"

The voice wasn't quite right. But it was close. Real close.

"Where's Cassel?" Sal said.

"Where indeed." Terrien smiled, his signature grin, the corners of his mouth turning up at the ends. "I thought you were coming alone." He was slightly annoyed, but the edges of the words were filled with pleasantries. Another Terrien trademark. Gentleness.

There were bandages and gauze along the lower left side of his face and part of an ear.

The door clicked shut behind us and then gas streams, thin waves, flushed from the switch plates of the room's four walls.

I couldn't see. My eyes filled with bee stings. The door was locked.

I wanted to blast my .38 but I was afraid of hitting Sal. Couldn't see him.

"What's going on? Terrien where are you?" Sal's voice was full of shadows.

"Nose filters," Terrien said, his voice drifting away from us. "Nose filters."

And the room got heavier and heavier, my lungs hurting as if blankets of flame were burning inside me.

And that's all I remember.

10

The world was off its axis and the spun cotton candy clotting my head had turned red. Red lint limned my eyes. The room was a dark, dark red and I wasn't sure if I was in a chair or even sitting down.

Terrien.

Gas.

Where was Sal?

Dr. Stangl, a hypodermic in his right hand, his eyes bright red coins, stood with his other hand inside his blood-colored lab coat. His face was hard to read in the clutter of reds that looked like a kid had let loose with his Spirograph.

I couldn't think right.

It was as if the walls in this room were made of dust, Roland-Garros red. Tennis anyone?

"Where is it?"

Gillian's voice. All of the soft, whimsical edges dissolving into hard elbows. When her lips moved I saw small coral snakes.

I was in a hardback chair. My hands and legs were free, but I didn't feel like I could lift them. "Where's what?"

The clay walls turned dark, earthen footlights. More Spirograph swirls. The whole setup looked like it was designed by Saul Bass.

"What Bobby left you." This time it was Airedale, his voice terse and thin, like a pack of weak firecrackers, not the kind that could blow off your hand. "Tell us—" He wasn't in a lab coat like Gillian. He was still the dedicated United Empire Loyalist in his blazer, now heavy red, with the three-pointed crown on the left breast. Behind him, looking at her shoes, was Leila, chips of hair peeking like angry birds from under her cap.

This was some fucking party.

And I had a killer hangover.

Not that I've ever been drunk. My father was an alcoholic, wearing sunglasses on days he was in a good mood, and I'd seen enough of his foul moods to never want to touch the stuff. But this felt like what a hangover must feel like. My head hurt like I'd fallen hard at center ice. And behind my eyes, a dull constant ache. Anacin wasn't going to help this shit. I blinked. The ache intensified.

"Where is it?"

I wasn't sure who asked this time. Did it matter?

The floor was a flood of red snakes.

I swam with their current.

WATER TRICKLED FROM a faucet like pulls of soft taffy. I was eight, maybe nine, mother had recently died, and it was my Saturday night ritual, a bath before the Leafs broadcast on radio with McClelland Stuart.

And then my father walked in, naked, hard in his hand.

The water looked like taffy.

"WHERE IS IT?"

That game again. I fluttered open my eyes, but the red was still there, flashing, bright, heavy, darker than the cherries on a police cruiser. "I don't know what you're fucking talking about."

Gillian leaned in, her breath full of coffee, dabs of Paris perfume on her neck. "The canisters? Three of them." Her face was an immobile mask.

That's why my house was broken into while the good doctor and I ate spaghetti at George's. "You owe me a mattress."

"Terry told us that Bobby left the bundle with you." I guess my client had brought them with him when he and the helicopter landed in my yard.

This was the first I'd heard of it. "So Terry was working for you too, huh? Why'd you whack him?"

"He had served his purpose." Airedale rubbed scruffy ends of his goatee.

"Who killed him?"

"No one you know." Airedale shrugged and pulled on the lapels of his blazer.

Gillian swallowed a half glass of water. I think it was water. It was odorless, but the color was a little off.

"No one I know, huh? Denys? Denys Goyette?"

Airdale rocked back slightly on his moccasins. It was a strange combo: the blazer, the wool pants, and moccasins with no socks. The no socks thing was a little gauche. I started laughing about the no socks thing. I couldn't help it.

"Denys doesn't use his hands," Gillian assured me, a thin smile creasing her lips.

I nodded. Denys. "A class act. He's got principles."

"Shut up." Airedale slapped me hard. As his hand knifed the room it resembled five flags flying in a hard wind. None of the flags were Canadian.

"Look, if Bobby left the junk with me, he didn't tell me." The cotton candy in my head was now bleeding through my nose and eyes. They must have pumped me full of Red 45, but if one of the side effects of the drug is forgetfulness why ask me to remember something that I've probably forgotten?

It takes several doses or an extreme dose for that side effect to kick in. Gillian assured me that what they gave me was minimal, just enough to loosen my inhibitions and get me to talk.

I had been talking out loud. Again. "Your version of the truth serum, huh?"

"Yes, a truth serum." Airedale, bored.

"Where's Terrien?"

Gillian's sexy charm and whimsy no longer had any fabric softener to it. She too was bored.

I guess I was a real pain in the ass. There I was drugged up, in a chair, listless, seeing all kinds of amoeba-shaped hallucinations, and I'm asking the questions.

"Yes, Fuller, you are a pain in the ass." Airedale rubbed the edge of his hand. I guess he hurt it when my face hit him.

"Terrien's resting comfortably." Gillian nodded.

Stangl, over her left shoulder, did something or other to the hypodermic, and it perspired. Leila was still studying her shoes. There weren't any snakes crawling across them. Gillian's shoes, on the other hand, were covered in thin snakes.

I think I hated her at that moment.

"Bobby didn't leave me a thing, except the conviction that he hadn't killed his wife. A conviction I share."

"Where are the canisters?" Airedale's goatee had turned to red dust.

When I was returning from the bathtub memories, my father, and taffy, I heard overlapping words, a rush and fall of frustrations. It seems the formula to Red 45 was lost or its original conception had been an accident, the compounds that went into its making forgotten. Some components came from rare South American extracts and plant resins. They could create new powders from the prototype, but the perfected mixture was impossible, it seems to re-attain. Guillame didn't take very good notes, apparently. Those 800 or so packets of Red 45 were the pure stuff. Everything else pales and lacks the killing power N'oublie jamais requires. Guillame was trying to find the right amount of elements, re-invent the old formula, but so far his efforts to recreate his work of accidental genius were limp. Bobby had stolen the best of what Guillame had to offer and they wanted it back.

"I'd rather die than give it to you fuckos."

That got me another slap.

This time from Gillian. She hit a hell of a lot harder than Baggy Ass.

If they didn't have the number-one stuff, the prime Red 45, what was this version doing to me?

"It may be watered down and not as potent, but it will let us know what we need to know," Gillian promised, her lips barely moving.

I inhaled, lungs full of flames. "Leila. What are you doing here? You're too nice a person to be mixed up with these yahoos."

She looked at her shoes. Now, they too, were covered with snakes.

The snakes slithering from my nose and mouth shifted sideways across the floor toward her shoes.

I closed my eyes. I hate snakes.

"Bobby didn't kill Nancy, did he, Cliff? Did he, Gillian? It was Terrien. That's why he had those bandages on his face when the gas spilled into that room. He was recovering from Nancy's counter punches. And she got in some good licks before she died." I smiled, eyes closed, breathing deeply, flames lashing my chest. "Only Terrien's not Terrien is he? Oh, no." I opened tired eyes, readying for more snakes. "Terrien was beaten to death three months ago in a garage. I was there. Saw his eye hanging out of his head, saw him take a last breath of bubblegum blood. Dawn saw Terrien but it wasn't the real Terrien, and that's why you wanted Dawn dead. Terrien's Cassel. You made him look like Spinner—you—"

It was rather simple, actually, Airedale gloated, playing with his goateed chin, left eyebrow raised like the back of a cat. "Their body structures were very similar." He paced behind my chair, hands locked. He smelled of Aqua Velva, the kind of aftershave I expected a cat like him to wear, swinger wannabe. The cool, mature cats like Migano wear Old Spice. Airedale bragged on and on about his work, his skill as a surgeon, how because they were both slight men with close-set eyes it was easy. Yes, the chin, the nose needed a lot of work, and some restructuring around the hairline, but overall it was a good match. And he was a great surgeon, highly skilled, top of his class at the U of T. Did I already tell you the highly skilled part? He must have mentioned it like eight times.

"And the voice." Gillian smiled. She couldn't resist joining the conversation. Doctors and their egos. Spinner had been interviewed twice on *Hockey Night in Canada* in the early '60s. They got Cassel archival tapes and had him practice the sound, rhythms, to Spinner's voice.

A regular Method actor he was.

Did Migano supply the archival tapes? He did win a video recorder in a high-stakes poker game. The person he won it from worked for the CBC.

CBC archived old games. My mind was firing, boychik, all cylinders.

So, Cassel got himself a fourth face. Terrien's dead and Cassel was going to use Spinner's face to begin life anew in

Oslo, Sweden.

"Oh, those plans have changed." Airedale missed my joke. "He's going away. Tomorrow. But he's not going there—"

"Quiet," Gillian chastised. "You're saying too much."

"Who cares, he won't live through the evening—"

"That's right." Gillian's kabuki face was faraway, all of its distanced artistry lost in Spirograph amoebas. "You should have—when I called you—you should have—said yes—"

"I don't live in should haves."

I did learn something from my therapist. The present is what matters, what I can do now. Don't live in the past.

Gillian looked over at Leila who was still studying her shoes. "We should keep our plans on the down-low, Cliff. There are other people present."

I wanted to re-tie Leila's laces.

I'm not sure why my mind went there but I wanted to untie and re-tie, untie and re-tie.

I started laughing again thinking about those laces. They looked like they belonged on the feet of a girl, a little girl.

And then I wanted to draw with Spirograph. I was a real mess. "Why did Cassel kill Nancy?"

"She knew too much about our operation." Airedale's voice was bathed in shrugs. "After she did that exclusive with that reporter, we couldn't take any more chances with follow-up conversations."

I blinked my eyes. The red wouldn't go away.

Talking to Stana numbered Nancy's days. If she could rat out Bobby, disclosing all of his sordid moments of domestic violence, what was to stop her from disclosing the secrets of N'oublie jamais? After all, she knew all of the players of this drama during her undergrad days at McGill. She was a Montreal girl. And from what I could gather, she didn't care for the whole lot of them.

"Yes. She was expendable and untrustworthy." Gillian folded her arms across her chest.

"She wasn't much of a lay either." Airedale smiled and motioned to Stangl.

He closed in. The tip of the needle perspired.

"I know nothing about the goddamn canisters—"

"The only reason you're still alive are those three canisters." Gillian's voice was full of blood.

"Where's Sal?"

I think I was screaming after that as the needle hit a vein and I hit the floor, my head landing hard at center ice, again, like taking a stick up high, a careless crosscheck, and I smelled wet leather, the undersides of hockey gloves, wet leather—

I STAGGERED ABOUT on my feet, unsure of how I got there or how to move my feet.

I kept talking to my feet. Move, damn it. And they did, like a baby walking for the first time, halting steps.

The hydrotherapy room.

And it wasn't white.

I didn't feel like a slalom skier fighting snow glare, because everything was red, but not the dark red of tinctured maple syrup, instead this was a brighter color, the landscape converted into Andy Warhol pop-art.

I don't care much for Andy Warhol.

Sal stood across from me. His arms swung in front of him, swaying axes. The ends of his beard were the red of a hot sun slipping beyond the horizon.

We didn't have a thing on.

Sal's arms kept swaying, as he leaned forward, the lower part of his face loose and jutted as if his jaw were unhinged.

A couple of old-school Greco–Roman wrestlers we were.

Nobody else was in the room. They must have been in the paneled windows above us, looking down, taking notes. Maybe they were even filming the event for Wide World of Sports.

Airedale's voice squawked across the intercom. It was the caw-caw of a crow with laryngitis.

Trust him to be unable to shut the fuck up. Mr. Soliloquy.

The doors were locked, he said. There was no exit.

And then he quoted John Donne.

I surveyed the room. A high ceiling, windows with bars, six tubs, with foam guns and nozzles for whirlpool comfort. Four shower stalls, open with sliding glass to our left, and the two locked exits with door handles that resembled submarine hatches.

He was still quoting Donne. He finally stopped. In five minutes, Airedale full of faux stentorian glee, said the Red 45 they had shot us full of will have taken effect and we will be transformed to our primordial ancestors and we will kill each other, like the story of the frog and the scorpion going across the lake and the scorpion needs the frog to get across but he stings him anyway and the two drown.

"I know the story," I shouted. Jesus Christ. Shut the fuck up.

"They drown, and when asked why? The scorpion said, 'Because it's my nature.'" He laughed. He just couldn't resist finishing stories. Some guys are real control freaks. "Your nature is to hunt, to gather, to kill. To tear off each other's faces."

That's what he was looking forward to, from this freak show that we were a part of. He laughed, caw-cawing as if fighting a cold.

To tell you the truth, I'd rather hear him quoting Donne.

But my thinking was solid. I hadn't reverted to an animal. I was still so cerebral, less instinctual. "I think we've come a long way since frogs and scorpions ruled the earth," I said.

"Droll, very droll. Mr. Fuller. Let's see who's laughing in five minutes."

No doubt, this was an experiment to see how potent their new improved Red 45 was.

Sweat formed across the top of Sal's upper lip and he snarled, the sounds coming up from deep inside him, and he lumbered toward me.

He definitely wasn't cerebral anymore.

I moved quickly, dancing, avoiding, running to the glass doors, then away from them, and toward the hydrotherapy tubs. I couldn't understand why Sal was transforming beyond a third face to a fourth, that of the primordial. Me, nothing much was happening to. My reflexes were still slow, I saw pink roses, and my arms weren't swaying.

At least the Spirograph amoebas were gone.

Sal tackled me and I fell hard, jarring my left shoulder, wincing from an old hockey injury. Sal was on top of me, fingers gouging my eyes. I twisted away from a stubby pressure that felt like the thumbs of heavy boxing gloves. I punched him hard on the chin and he fell to the floor before springing back up.

My punch ought to have done more damage than that. Shit.

He came at me again, the curled hairs of his chest matted to his skin, those arms swaying axes.

Why wasn't I filled with hate?

He was? Why not I?

We grappled with the back of each other's necks, his hands hooks, scratching, tearing, tine fork lines across my skin, like Bobby's face, and pictures of Nancy, and I tried talking to Sal, we don't have to do this, but his rational id had punched the clock, breaking it, minutes ago.

His hands stiffened around my neck.

My lungs were tongues of flame.

And I felt my father's hands on my neck, as he pushed my face into the bed, and told me to stay quiet, this wouldn't hurt, and this is how we show our love, a secret kind of love, the room full of beer and cigarettes, his fingers like Sal's fingers, boxing gloves.

"Sal." I stomped on the instep of one of his feet. He let go, and the then I kneed him, hard, in the crotch. He collapsed like a heavy canvas feed sack. I ran for the hydrotherapy tub. A foam gun. I was David and this was my Goliath stone. Shit, I hope the water's turned on. It was.

The foam gun jittered in my hands.

Sal clambered to his feet, arms swaying.

He raced toward the gun.

I fired. Foam, ropes of soap suds, arced the air and he stumbled and fell, tangled in the slippery mess.

With my other hand I reached for the spray gun and alternated blast after blast of the two weapons, at his chest, propelling him back, farther back, and he toppled, hitting his head on the edge of one of the tubs, ropes of foam all around him.

He wasn't moving.

I swayed and fell in the foamy suds and laughed. I laughed. And laughed.

And then I wondered who it was who was laughing because it didn't feel like me anymore.

I WOKE UP and I could smell it. Turpentine. Paint.

There was no chair. Just me and a mattress. I was in their secret lab, the one on the drop floor. Where was Sal?

A door opened followed by light that glinted and then died.

The red was almost an orange and yellow now. My eyes didn't hurt as much when I blinked them or held them shut.

Airedale, his blazer now a completely different color, the three-crowns on his breast as pointed as ever, wobbled into the room, limping like a twisted letter "I." Behind him, Leila, carrying a tray with two hypodermics, cotton swabs, gauzes and tape.

"Well, that didn't quite go as we expected, now did it?" He was talking as if giving yet another soliloquy. He was no Edmund.

But I was feeling a little bit like Lear. "Sorry to disappoint," I said. The new Red 45 wasn't up to the old standards.

"Both of you should be dead."

"Uh-huh. I guess the litmus paper for your little experiment turned blue instead of red, huh?"

"Humor, Mr. Fuller. Really?"

"It's nice to see I have clothes on today." It was the first time I noticed. I was in hospital scrubs.

"Your resistance interests me, Mr. Fuller. Sal turned primordial. You didn't? Why? What kind of will power do you have?"

"Willpower? Shit. I never finished a crossword puzzle in my life—"

"Let's see how strong your will is."

"Another test?"

He pointed at the tray in Leila's arms. Two needles. One full of enough Red 45 to turn me into an ape-man, possibly causing me to kill myself, as if I were the scorpion and the frog rolled into one. The other needle Heroin. Pure. Uncut. Mainline that and I'd be dead within minutes. Which of the two will I choose? He tapped his chin, grinned and nodded. His nose looked slick in the orange light. "I'm providing you with a possible exit strategy." He threw back his head and laughed.

I suspected that the heart of this experiment was to see if a person under enough Red 45 could actually tear himself to death.

The way these sickos got their kicks.

"Yes, kicks." Another laugh. He smiled. "Think over your options. I'll be back in five." He laughed again and told Leila to watch me until he returns. He left the room.

Leila pulled out a gun. It was my snub-nosed .38. I recognized the grip tape on the handle and nick on the barrel's edging.

I sat on the mattress.

Leila held the tray. Option A or B.

"What would you choose to do," I said, thinking myself a regular smart-ass.

"Fight. And get out of here."

"Huh?"

She smiled, her lips parting slightly, and she nudged close the door behind her. The Red 45 she had been administering to me was a low, low dose. It was primarily saline solution.

"That's why the red migraines haven't been as dark as—"
She nodded.

The room was yellow-orange right about now. But Sal, he had been given the full treatment.

"Yes," she mumbled, looking away. "I never thought they'd have the two of you fight." She shook her head. "I'm sorry I put you to such a disadvantage." Her voice was no longer a whisper lost in a tunnel.

"Is Sal still alive?"

He was. After finishing with me, they were about to make him the same offer. Only Sal wasn't in his right mind. He was lost, full of primordial wanderings and incomprehensible mumbling. And he couldn't remember a god-damn thing.

By contrast, the low dose of drugs caused me to remember a lot of things, things I had repressed, forced away, incidents with my father that I wanted to confess to her, encounters that ended once I reached puberty and got stronger, excelling at hockey.

The game gave me autonomy, control over my body.

"You're nowhere as weak as Cliff expects you to be," she said. "Use that to your advantage." Yes, the hypodermic on the left of the tray was a suicide bomb, pure heroin, but that on the right wasn't full of Red 45, but enough of a knockout elixir to render someone unconscious for hours. Her plan: when Airedale returns stab him with the hypo.

"What if he has company?"

She pointed at the gun in her hand.

"Why not just give me the goddamn gun?"

"Because it's empty." No one else knew the gun was empty but Cliff. "Cliff didn't trust me with a loaded gun, but he figured you wouldn't risk it."

"This is fucked up."

"You want to know what's fucked up?"

I was surprised by her language. I liked it. "What's fucked up?"

They filmed our fight, mine and Sal's, from the Opticon room upstairs. All the time, Dr. Williams sat forward in her chair, fingertips by her mouth, lips parted as if she were anticipating a car wreck at Indy, like Sad Eddie Sachs, remember, dying in a ball of flame?

I remembered.

They filmed murder to get their kicks.

"Where's Cassel?"

He had left the country. And he wasn't going to Sweden. Some other undisclosed place was his destination where he could begin a new life with a new identity. Argentina, Brazil, maybe? Singapore? She wasn't sure. She'd been listening for hints but Airedale and Williams were pretty closed-mouth about it all.

I gave her a look. "Is he really gone, this time?"

She nodded.

"You ever see Denys? The guy in the photo you showed me, the guy with a fleur-de-lis tattoo under his left eye. Lambskin hat?"

All the time. Comes in often around closing. Talks to Gillian, possibly plotting the next moves for N'oublie jamais.

"Did Bobby tell you what he was going to do with the canisters?"

"I hoped you would tell me."

"Is that why you're helping me?"

She reached into her lab coat and flashed her credentials. "I'm RCMP. Undercover." Anne Chevalier was her real name. She was from Quebec City and had been infiltrating N'oublie jamais for months. She was the one in the silver Corvair, gray in the sun, following me. It was she who fed me additional information about Dawn Stoukas, sending photographs of her and Terry to Stana's *Toronto Telegram* location.

"All to get me to help you, to be part of your mission—"

"Yes."

"I don't like the games the RCMP plays, Anne. I could've got killed."

"A whole lot of other people could get killed, if not for—" Look, we need those canisters, to stop them from falling into enemy hands, she said. They can't duplicate the formula, but what they have created, and Bobby may have hid, those lost prototypes are deadly. Yes, she used me, but for the greater good. She had tried to minimize the risks.

"Minimize? What do you call those low-risk hijinks in the hydrotherapy room, a friendly wrestling match?"

"That was a variable I didn't see coming."

But if I had been pumped full of Red 45 both Sal and me would be dead, faceless.

"Yes. I wasn't sure what side you were on. If you had the canisters would you sell them?"

"You don't know me very well," I said.

"What I'm getting to know, I like." She smiled. It was pretty and disarming.

Airedale re-entered the room. He had a jaunty appearance as if he had just got laid. Maybe he had. "What did you decide?"

"Red 45? What else?"

"Good." The other option, massive cardiac arrest was too easy. He appreciated how I entered into the sport of it all, my fight, my willingness to not be conquered but accept defeat nonetheless. It was another damn soliloquy.

He motioned Leila to administer the hypo and adjusted a loose button on his blazer, undid it, tucked in his shirt, hitched his pants, re-adjusted the blazer. He *did* just get laid. Him and Gillian, no doubt.

Leila lifted the hypo from the tray and stabbed Airedale in the chest with it. His hands stuttered and his eyes turned filmy as he reached for her face, thumb in her mouth, hand slipping on her shoulders, and as his fingers flitted, he flopped down her hips, to the floor. I smelled shit.

"Well, that's rather unfortunate," I said.

"God, he would never shut up," Anne said.

I laughed. No one would ever say Airedale's soliloquies would rival those of Hamlet.

"I'm going with you," Anne announced.

"I figured on that once you went all John Wayne with the needle."

I also figured it was my fight, but Anne figured differently. These were scientists. How long before they realized the switches she was making in the doses she administered to me? How long before they figured out the knockout hypo? It was too risky to stay undercover.

I smiled and said let's find Sal.

"Room six," she said.

Airedale snored loudly into his shoulder. The sound was a frayed serpentine belt.

We hurried down the long, low-ceilinged lab to the green door at the end. Green. I actually saw the color. Green, not yellow-orange. I was coming out of it. "You know we did background checks on you, Nancy's alleged sister?"

"When the RCMP gives you a cover story it's a good one."

Damn straight. Unlike my attempt to be Hawley Walker, king of the thoroughbreds, the RCMP knew their shit.

"You're a good actor, Anne. I mean, mousy girl, all retreating and shit, and now the voice of confidence, a kick-ass professional who just gave Baggy Ass one hell of a sleeper move. Look out Whipper Billy Watson."

She looked at me.

"Professional Wrestling?"

The look intensified.

"Never mind."

It felt good to take him down, she said. She wasn't trying to challenge my manhood or anything, she just got sick of the guy's bluster. Plus, he looked like a scientist from a bad 1950s movie.

That just cracked me up. Maybe I *was* finally coming around.

We ran down the hall. It was dim and the runners faintly bled red.

Anne gave me back my empty gun, but I really wanted

my porkpie.

I'll buy you a new one, she said.

I stumbled against her shoulder and over her feet as we darted along the walls. Her feet looked like a twist of red snakes. I guess the after effects of the drugs hadn't completely worn off.

Sal was in a lot worse shape than me.

If his injections were at the same low level as mine, Gillian and Cliff would surely have gotten suspicious and Anne's cover would be blown. But Sal. In his purple room, with a bookshelf, bed, chair and lamp, just sat limp in his chair, shoulders slumped, eyes unfocused. He was like that old tom cat, Dawn described, the one you waited too long to fix and after you did it just perched atop the TV mindlessly staring.

"Sal, Sal."

I wondered if his world were still filled with red footlights.

I nudged and pushed, but I couldn't get him off the chair he was anchored to. His scrubs had dried spittle on them. A line of sweat, perforated licorice, dotted his upper lip.

"Let me." Anne injected Sal with whatever was in the hypo in her lab coat. He collapsed into her chest within seconds. She eased him to the floor, and seizing the back of his collar, dragged him down the narrow hallway, the runner lights, blinking black, every time Sal's massive form passed by.

We got to the end of the hall, the door. It opened soundlessly.

The side street was dark with conical light splashed here and there. It was cool for July, the night air brightening my face. I was drowning in the air, a good kind of drowning, I gulped in more of it.

She glanced up and down the street and said something

or other about having a gun in her car. "Wait here."

"What did you mean before when you said you weren't sure you could trust me?"

"What?"

"Back in the lab. You said, you weren't sure you could trust me—"

Well, I did make a name for myself taking photos of people having affairs, didn't I, she said. It's kind of a dirty business. Divorce work.

I nodded.

"And all for what?" She exhaled sharply. It had got me drummed out of the NHL didn't it? "Why do it, why?"

"A Hi-Fi unit," I said.

Her smile was slightly broken off. She promised to be right back.

I breathed in more deeply, the flames in my lungs losing some of their tongues. Leila. That was her fourth face. A reticent, scared woman, vulnerable, the kind of woman I feel a need to protect. But Anne was strong, in control. Knew her shit.

Cassel. His fourth face was Terrien. I'm sure he had Terrien's social identification card, readying to take on the identity of a person so unlike himself, a kind person, a person who had to scratch and fight for every chance he ever got in the NHL. And now Cassel was somewhere in South America. Or Singapore. Cassel. As a kid, the myth was that the RCMP always got its man. I sure hope they catch up with that creep someday.

Anne was six cars down, leaning into her Corvair. The dim light from a nearby Becker's backlit her shoulders.

The sky was black asphalt. Sal was crumpled up against my knees. He looked odd and lost in his hospital scrubs. I wanted to get him back in his Sloan Wilson grays.

I don't have a lot of friends.

Sal was one of the few.

From the shadows emerged a tall, lanky form, Sgt. Jack Moffat, his brown fedora pushed back rakishly.

"Moffat—"

He reached inside his brown blazer and two shots, sounding as if they were one, nails hammered rapidly, had Moffat falling sideways to the street, his hat tumbling, landing upside down on a manhole cover.

Anne walked into the light, breathing heavily, her pistol low on her right side. She stood over his body. Gray matter was on the street. "He was the mole," she said. "He was going to kill you. You and Sal."

There was a gun by his cold fingers. She was a hell of a shot. Moffat went down like a marionette that had its strings cut.

Moffat had killed Officer Sarah Linney, his partner. She had been working undercover for the RCMP, digging up dirt on Moffat, filling file folders with information on his ties with N'oublie jamais.

"Moffat? Isn't that an English name?"

"You don't have to be French to be a traitor." Anne re-holstered her pistol.

I nodded. Sirens filled the sky.

Moffat, Anne said, had set up Sarah for the hit. He was the one who opened the curtains. He was the one who contacted Goyette with her location. She was the target all along. It was never about Dawn.

The sirens overlapped, concussing through the night's stillness.

Soon the curtain would fall on Adora Borealis.

Fall?

I wanted to burn down their whole fucking theatre of operations. God knows they had enough turpentine and paint in that place to make it burn. All of them inside, including my father, laughing, while burning red, burning bright.

Christ.

And I started crying.

Anne hugged me.

She smelled of the night. Flowers blooming at night. I guess that's what her name means in Hebrew, night, and something about that made me laugh a little through the tears.

She strengthened her hold.

I hadn't been loved this way in a long, long time.

 was out for three days and then, like Lazarus, I was back.

No more migraines.

And Stana was with me.

She fed me soup, helped me get to and from the bathroom, and listened to my teeth chatter as I went through withdrawal.

My body was always cold and my skin looked like a fish's underbelly.

I slept on the couch.

Adora Borealis was shut down. The police and the RCMP found enough stuff to indict Airedale, Williams, and Stangl on more charges than the Leafs had Stanley Cup rings. Kidnapping, attempted murder (mine and Sal's), sedition and trafficking. Dawn Stoukas and a host of other "lab workers" agreed to testify against the clinic and its manufacturing of illegal drugs. The RCMP found traces of black market hallucinogens in both labs. A chemical analysis revealed that the powders were made up of a compound of LSD and several rare components from plant life. Only five of the eight elements in the drug samples could be identified. No wonder, N'oublie jamais wanted those 800 or so packets back. They had no idea what some of the rare elements, rosins and extracts, were. A search of

Airedale's office uncovered a half-ass outline of Guillame's plans for Expo '67, including a rather elaborate analysis of how Montreal's water filtration operates, and just how much Red 45 would be needed to mess up the system.

Cliff Airedale and "Dr." Stangl were in police custody awaiting their preliminary hearing. Indictments would follow.

Dr. Gillian Williams was a no-show. A dragnet had been dropped on the city and somehow she had slipped through. N'ouble jamais had her, in hiding, somewhere between here and Montreal.

Sal was still in the hospital, suffering from some kind of form of combat fatigue.

He couldn't remember a damn thing involving the last two weeks of his life.

Anne Chevalier had checked up on me a couple of times in the past three days to see how I was doing. Both times she wore Capri pants, a tan-colored blouse, and moved about my living room with long, brisk strides, as if she were just finishing up eighteen holes of golf. Her face was fresh-scrubbed, no makeup. I wanted to ask her out for a cup of coffee, but she was probably due to get re-stationed someplace, like the Yukon or something, chasing Dangerous Dan McGrew.

And Gray Davies, the guy who died in the car wreck, Guillame's lab assistant? He lived with Guillame for two years, in an apartment they shared, Stana said.

"Bachelors or lovers?"

"It could go either way—"

"Wow."

"You look better." Stana's hair was pulled back in a long ponytail. She wore slacks and a blouse. She lit a Parliament.

"I feel better. Lots better." A red blanket covered me. I was still a little cold. My feet in wool socks were up on a low-riding coffee table.

"I guess I should get going pretty soon. Back to work. Tomorrow maybe." Her lips parted slightly as she spoke, a trace of lipstick dotted the end of her cigarette.

It was late in the afternoon, my backyard a shimmer of blue lake.

I reached for her wrist and gave it a pat. "I appreciate you being here. Watching over me."

She smiled. "I want to stay your friend—"

We'd had a major falling out on my last case. "You are my friend."

"I know we can't go back to where we were before but—"

"Friends?"

"Friends." She took another drag and smothered a short laugh. "I guess I should have asked if I could smoke before I lit up—"

I shifted on the couch, part of my ass was numb, and my left shoulder, from my fight with Sal, was no longer as tight as it was yesterday. I could at least raise my arm above my head. "It's fine." I always liked the smell of cigarettes, the heavy curtain of Rothman's, which my father and Sal smoked, to the lighter, Venetian blinds of an Export A or a Parliament.

"Sal should be leaving the hospital today," Stana said.

"Good. He's all right?"

She shook her hand, fingers stuttering. "Comme ci, comme ca."

I loved the freckles to her eyes, the line between her eyebrows that furrowed when she concentrated, the stern set to her jaw when she's mad, the gentleness of her full lips. "I was abused—"

I just said it. I didn't think. I just said it.

She knew about the abuse, how my father loved to hang me over a balcony in Scarborough, fourteen floors up from the street, or how he left me abandoned for several hours in a car, window cracked, while he tossed darts in the neighborhood bar, or how he smacked me about for whatever he failed at in life: work, marriage, being a father.

We flew kites together, watched hockey, strolled Balmy Beach. Those were the good times. There weren't many.

Stana knew all that. She placed her burning cigarette on the lip of an ashtray parked next to a folded-over copy of *The Hockey News*.

"No. I don't mean just that way."

We didn't say anything. The smell of the cigarette lingered, suddenly pungent.

And now she really knew.

She moved between the coffee table and couch, hugging me, tears warming our faces.

I guess I needed her to understand that that was why, or possibly why, there was a part of me that held back in our relationship, that couldn't give my all. During sex I feared letting go, as if giving of myself completely to her would be a surrender. I needed to protect myself. Always. There was so much armor covering me, a heavy chain mail of jokes, ironic quips, smart-ass zingers, keeping me from being totally present and mindful. And maybe the abuse accounts for why I was so mediocre in bed.

"You weren't mediocre." She looked away.

"You can't even look at me when you say it. I wanted our love to be passionate. Not sweet." She told me it was nice, sweet, the last time. "B+. That's the best I could ever do with you, B+."

"Don't reduce yourself to a letter grade."

"B+."

"Okay. That seems about fair." She smiled and kissed me on the cheek. "but that's a really good grade." She laughed, wiping tears from the corners of my eyes. Then she kissed my forehead. I wiped tears from her face. She kissed me gently on the lips. "I'm so sorry this happened to you—"

And then we both cried.

"Hey, hey—" I reached for her hands. "It was a relief to tell you."

"How long did it go on?"

"I'm not sure." I looked at my fingers. One of the nails was torn, just like a nail on Bobby's hand after whatever happened on the night Nancy died. "I was eight, nine, ten." I shrugged. "After a while, I didn't count."

She wondered if I were going to confront my father about this. He was living somewhere in Scarborough.

I planned to.

See Dr. Cohen first, talk it over with her, seek her advice.

I planned to do that too.

"Oh, Hayden—"

She rested her head between my shoulder and neck.

It made me happy.

And we stayed like that for forty-five minutes or so, watching the early newscast on CBC.

I shifted once again.

"You need to pee?"

She'd got me one of those cylinder things from a hospital so I wouldn't have to walk to the bathroom as often. It was difficult to move, my back still felt like it was wrapped in chains. "No, no. I'm good." I smiled. It was pleasing to smile when you knew someone cared about you. "Lower desk drawer. Left hand side."

Stana moved a lot like Anne: brisk, compact, athletic.

The drawer stuttered and she lifted the manila envelope, undid the clasp, and pulled out five 8x10s. She studied them as if looking at an American cousin who only visits Canada every two-three years. "Wow. I was something."

"You still are." My lips were rubber bands, loosening. "I

want you to have them back—"

She wasn't ashamed of these photographs. I had captured the fun, playful, sexy side to her, a side that wasn't very present these days. "Keep them, Hayden."

I'm not sure that that was what I wanted to hear.

Mementoes weren't for me. "Sure, sure."

"God, I was so young back then." She took a quick puff off her Parliament. "And my ass hadn't started to fall—"

"Your ass is great—"

"And you, obviously, aren't fully recovered. You're still seeing a lot of red."

"Don't make me laugh or I will need to piss."

"Go ahead."

So I did, sitting on the couch, spraying into the container. When I finished she took it away.

The way I keep desiring a return to Stana, wanting her to come back, to love Stana. Is that a sign of someone who suffers from sexual abuse? An inability to let go and move on, just like I felt I needed my father? Is it healthy to still want Stana after what happened on the prior Stabulas case?

She returned and we watched *Combat!* on ABC. I couldn't wait for the new fall season to start, *Honey West*.

"You just like Anne Francis," she said.

"What's not to like," I said, and then I looked down at my half-torn off fingernail from my fight with Sal and I knew why Bobby, on the night I saw him, looked like he had fallen into a barb-wired fishing net.

TWO HOURS LATER, around nine p.m., the sky outside was a dark harvest red, and Babe Migano strolled into my living room, jousting on the balls of his feet. He wore a pinstripe suit, and the rose in his lapel was jousting too.

"I don't usually make house calls, shamus, but Stana called me. Said you wanted to get a message to Bobby." He sat by my side in a leather chair, removed his hat, and balanced it on a knee. He smelled of Old Spice. None of that flashy Aqua Velva shit for him. "How you doing, Stana?"

"I'm good, Babe." She looked away.

"Good, good. That article you wrote about unfair wages for women—" He pointed a finger that was a series of rings that resembled a scorpion's tale. "My niece loved. Said it was about time. A real woman's libber, that broad."

"How's Athol?" I interrupted, a slight edge to my voice.

"You're being a little salty, shamus. And you're making me sensitive again." He smiled, his face glowing with the confidence of a music-hall impresario. "Just to ease your mind. There's nothing going on between me and Stana. That's over."

They had been partners in the past, planting evidence, setting me up to discover overdetermined outcomes. False leads under a toupee.

Stana nodded, unable to look at either one of us. "Over." It was a very quiet utterance full of mild conviction.

"Athol?" Babe shrugged. "Let's just say he's no longer driving the yellow Buick." That car was a block and a half long.

"He's dead?"

"No." Babe wiped away a laugh with the back of a hand. "Like I said, he's no longer driving the car. It's all Lou, 24–7."

Lou Fortunado. Babe's other bodyguard. "Where's Lou?" I missed our fine chatter about the latest plays in Toronto's burgeoning theatre scene.

"He's in love. Typical fella. Head over heels about some doll and the boys never see him anymore. Doesn't shoot pool. Doesn't bowl—"

I nodded.

Athol, bowler in his hands, apologized to Babe for moonlighting, making side money. He knew Cassel in the

American Hockey League. They played in Providence, for a while, roommates on the road, before Athol got the call-up with Boston. Anyway, while holed up in Adora Borealis, Cassel got in touch with Athol, and one conversation led to another, and Athol confessed to beating Brian "Spinner" Terrien to death, on orders from me, Migano, and how they threw his body in a field, and that's when Cassel decided to become Terrien. They had similar bone structure. Drs. Airedale and Williams agreed and performed the plastic surgery and now Cassel's walking this land as Terrien.

Just great. Terrien becomes a fourth face for a sadistic piece of shit like Cassel.

Migano shrugged. "I know it." But it was a guilt we all three have to carry. We know the truth. I saw Terrien die. Stana, accidently, set up the death. Neither of us could report it because Babe would kill us. So all three of us keep breathing, living this horrible lie, while a faux Terrien walks, possibly, alongside us.

"It doesn't seem right. A nice guy like Terrien inhabited by Cassel," Stana said.

"Right or not that's how the dice rolled," Babe said. He leaned forward in his chair. The leather squeaked a little. Hank Mobley with Philly Joe Jones on drums was playing the last set at White Heat. He had to catch it, so let's hurry things along.

"Hank Mobley?" I was jealous. I wanted to join Babe for the set, but Stana said no, I was still pissing in a container. I was in no condition to go out.

"Well, you two sure have got comfortable with one another again." Migano glanced back and forth between us.

"We're just friends," she said.

"And I'm just a businessman." He laughed and pointed the finger crowded with rings at me. "It's funny when I make that joke. You make it, Hayden, and I get sensitive."

He laughed again. "Ever find that cache of Red 45?"

"No," I said.

"What message do you want me to get to Bobby?"

"Tell him he didn't kill Nancy. Cassel did. Airedale and Gillian practically admitted as much when Cliff was threatening to shoot me up with Red 45." I rubbed the edges of my mouth. "You know how people get when they think you're about to take your final taxi? They bloviate, go on and on."

Airedale was a pretentious set of bag pipes.

Anyway, my teeth were sore and my body cold. I pulled the blanket around me tightly. You, see, Babe, it was partial payment for the surgery, a kind of sick experiment. They wanted to see how powerful the drug was, how much it loosened up inhibitions and filled our receptors with enough anger and hate to bring about action. Nancy was being difficult and she knew too much. She'd become expendable after she'd talked to Stana. Maybe she was going to tell Stana more than what they wanted out there. The kicker. They filmed it. I'm pretty sure. Gillian's into that, she gets her sexual kicks out of hurting, killing people. If I could just get my hands on that film. Anyway, Bobby, medicated on Blue 27, must have stumbled on Cassel's kill at Nancy's apartment. Remember now, Bobby out of his own sickly obsessions or need to protect Nancy had been following her. On the night she was murdered Bobby stumbled upon Cassel, out of his mind on Red 45, killing Nancy, that's why Bobby was all cut-up, his fingernail torn off. He didn't get those wounds from Nancy warding him off to save her own life. No, he got those wounds from Cassel, fighting Bobby off, trying to save his miserable life. I held up my broken fingernail. I got this from tangling with Sal, and we hardly grappled at all. Bobby's fight with Cassel lasted a while, a long while. Unfortunately, Bobby has no memory of the night in question, a side effect of the drugs, but once he experiences some recall, lookout!

"Shit." Babe exhaled sharply, his shoulders slightly shaking.

"Cassel killed Nancy. But in a way Gillian did. She made Cassel into an experimental hit man." And they were there. Filming it all.

"You won't be able to prove it unless Bobby's memory returns," Babe said.

I touched my forehead. It was cold. "Or unless I get that goddamn film. But that's how I see it."

"You've proved it to me," Babe said.

"It sounds pretty convincing," Stana agreed. When all the arrows of a case point in one direction, chances are you need to break some of the arrows and twist them so they point elsewhere.

That's my theory and I'd been sharing it with her all afternoon. "Tell Bobby." He can quit living with fear, guilt.

"I will." Babe patted my shoulder. I could sit in his hand—It was that big. "This will make him happy." He stood up. "You feel a little cold, Hayden, you okay?"

"Yeah, yeah." It felt like winter in here for chrissakes. I wanted a second blanket.

"Me and Stana may have had a brief thing a while back, but she always talked about you. When she was with me, she was with you." He lifted his black fedora from his knee, put it on, and was gone.

"Oh, hell, hell." Stana ambled toward the desk, resting a hip against it. She picked up the manila envelope. "I can't be this person again, Hayden. She's gone."

"Who says I even want you to be that person?" I couldn't follow her to the desk. I wanted to, to hug her, kiss her, but I was too cold to move. "That person is a part of you now, but you're no longer her. I love both of those people—"

"Your teeth are chattering—"

"Must be love." I laughed weakly.

She brought me another blanket, and a third. She tucked it around me, the freckles in her eyes, sad.

I smiled meekly and slipped into a rigid lake, my face trapped for air somewhere between the black cold beneath me and the layer of ice above.

WHEN I AWOKE, Stana sat next to me, her face, what I could see of it, full of concern, her lips downturned. "Maybe I should stay a couple of more days." She laughed gently. She could go to work but come back in the evenings. I wasn't doing so hot.

I was actually feeling a lot better than a few hours ago, but I didn't want to ruin any suggestion that would keep her around longer. She made even watching Ed Sullivan fun.

"Yeah. That would be great." The room was dark. Slight shadows from streetlights filled out a corner of the coffee table and the side of Stana's face. A pulse line ran through her jaw.

"What was it you liked about me, the first moment you saw me?" She touched my arm.

"Your freckles." They had this random chaos, like so many atoms moving at once, glowing, suggesting all kinds of contradictions and fun possibilities. There was an energy to Stana that I was drawn to, still am, an uncertainty to the movements of her freckles, suggesting that no one moment would ever be the same. I tried to put all that into words and since she was smiling I figured I had said something nice and complimentary. My mind wasn't working so good, and I couldn't express myself as clearly as I usually could.

"I noticed in my pictures, the freckles, you always

brought them out."

I nodded. "Like I said, I have a thing for freckles."

She laughed. "I can't believe you talked me into posing."

"Yeah." I laughed faintly under her words.

"You wanted to test out the equipment, see how well it works, before you started working cases—"

"Right. All very reasonable."

"Right, reasonable. Uh-huh. And you needed me naked to—"

"To, uh, make sure I had the contrasts set right." Filming a woman in clothes was much different, in terms of lighting, from filming her naked. After all, I was working divorce cases. Skin tone, right?

"Right. I'm sure the variables between shooting clothes and the human body are different." She turned, her shoulders backlit with streetlight. A smile filled her eyes. "And do you remember that crazy idea you had to shoot me in infrared? That was just a little too kinky."

It was a kind of a gimmicky lens, sentimental. Stana had a point, but—

I pinched my eyes shut. "Infrared—"

"What—"

Bobby, when he was last here, looked a couple of times in the mirror, world weary, tracing the lines of his tired face, unhappy with what he saw. But what if he were tracing something else? "Help me get to the bedroom."

She guided my steps as if we were crossing a rickety, roped bridge in some South American dictatorship. I grabbed my camera from between the wall and bed, set the f-stop to 1.4, and twisted in place the infrared lens. I motioned for her to shut off all the lights.

Bobby *wasn't* tracing the lines in his face.

Bobby was writing words, dry soapy streaks, scratched against the mirror.

In the bald grass.

I motioned for Stana to look through the Leica's viewfinder.

"In the bald grass," she repeated. "What the fuck's that mean?" She turned on the lights. The words disappeared. "Invisible ink?"

"Invisible ink," I echoed. Bobby did bring the Red 45 here, not on my premises, but the house to the left, the one with no grass, *bald grass.*

"Why didn't he just give you the shit?"

"I don't know." He didn't trust me, I guess, not completely, so he was speaking in a metaphoric code. Maybe if he gave the stuff directly to me, I'd make the wrong choice, too soon. Getting seeped in the case, got me thinking right.

I slid into a pair of Keds and breathed deeply. The flames had left my lungs.

Stana did up the top buttons on my pajamas and kissed me.

"I also liked how you care about people. That attracted me to you, Stana. The stories you wrote for the *Telegram.* You write about underdogs. Women being mistreated. You write about our shared need for social justice—"

This time I kissed her.

She seemed to like it.

But I wasn't going to allow myself to get confused over our relationship. If only she'd have agreed to take the nude photos. That would have been a sign that we could move forward romantically, that she wasn't leaving me with leftovers to remember her by.

I better talk to Dr. Cohen, make sure it was all right to have this rush of feelings for Stana, make sure I wasn't following a pattern I needed to be free of.

There's a lot of things I need to be free of.

I played with her ponytail, lifting it from the back of her

neck. "You want to find a treasure?"

"Yes."

We grabbed a flashlight.

It took only twenty minutes.

There was a patch of earth, not as dry and gray as the rest. We dug black dirt with our hands. I'd forgotten a shovel. The earth pushed and nudged under my fingernails.

All three canisters were there.

We unscrewed the lids. Condom-like packages pressed up against the insides of the cylinders. It was like a red sky and it was all you could see.

I squeezed her arm, between wrist and elbow. The moon above us was a flipped omelet. Two or three lights were lit on the block. "We got it, Stana, we got it."

"Easy, Hayden, you're hurting me."

"We've got it. Goddamn it, we've got it."

12

The air circling my face, cool then warming, as I came out of a light sleep, sensing some presence in the leather chair next to me.

A bundle of formless rocks breathed gently in the shadows. The mass gently rubbed its chin. Bobby.

"Hey, shamus."

My eyes were sewn open.

The clock on the coffee table read 2:10. It's fifteen minutes fast. I pinched my eyes shut and blinked away bits of grit. Stana was off in the bedroom. I heard gentle sighs, rising and falling.

I couldn't see much of Bobby's face. The night was a series of darker and darker triangles, diagonal shadows, that only revealed a corner of the coffee table, an arm on the leather chair, a spot on the floor. The marks on Bobby's right hand, the one gripping the chair's armrest, had more or less healed over.

"Babe told me you wanted to see me. Something to do with Nancy's death." He repeated what I had told Babe. Bobby's nose in black-angled light looked different, smaller, the bump of a hawk, gone.

"Yeah. That's exactly what I told him." Not quite, but I wasn't going to quibble over a few minor details.

"I knew something wasn't quite right." He took in a deep

breath. He struggled to fill his lungs. I wondered if he were still feeling the after effects from his fight with Cassel.

"What do you mean?"

Aside from the plastic bag and Nancy's bulging eyes, he couldn't remember a single detail of the scuffle. But much later, as of two days ago, small little pockets of memory filled him with dread, as he remembered sitting on a loveseat in Nancy's apartment, Gillian and Airedale, leaning into each other's shoulders while telling him the horrors of what they saw, how Bobby had tried to lift Nancy's head from her neck. They had it all on film and he better take the boarding pass they handed him to a boat bound for Sweden. They knew a captain of this merchant ship. It was docked in Montreal. "'You don't ever want to see that film,' they told me."

"Why were they in the apartment, Nancy's apartment in the first place?"

He stretched his fingers. They were spiderwebs. "Getting her reaction on film to a new drug—"

"Jouissance?"

"Yeah."

I didn't say anything else.

"It was supposed to be a woman's drug or something—"

Or something. "I'd like to see that film." I sat forward on the couch. "It was Cassel. They lied to you, Bobby."

"How can you be so sure?"

"The lines on his face. That's how." I placed my hand by my pillow. My snub-nosed .38 was a stretch of fingers away. "Cassel's need for follow-up plastic surgery. That's how. And Airedale confessed as much, suggesting Cassel was the killer, when he thought I was about to checkout, tear off my own face and die from an overdose of Red 45."

He nodded, the bottom half of his face rearranged, sunset puzzle pieces fit into puzzle pieces for a cool lunar surface.

"Think about it, man, think about that night. What really happened? Not that story they concocted and brainwashed you with—Think back—" Cassel was in the room, attacking Nancy. You were following her, came upon the attack, tried to stop it—

He smiled, lips raw liver, heavier than I remembered. "That makes a nice story. Me as hero, trying to rescue her." He shook his head. "But I'm no hero. She died. And even if I didn't kill her, I could have easily done it all those other times I had beaten her with these fists." He held up his hands. They were no longer full of barb-wire scratches. "I'm guilty all the same."

He had created an environment of abuse he said.

Yes, I nodded, you had. The photographs Stana tossed my way a week ago, the ones with Nancy and chipped teeth, swollen face, pouchy eyes, and missing hair corroborated Bobby's presumption of guilt.

"That's what happens when you have time to think, Hayden. I hurt her. Again and again." He cried gently, his mouth quavering. "You find the stuff?"

"Yeah. I gave it to the RCMP." I lied. I had three cylinders hidden in my bedroom closet, in a hockey duffel bag, full of old gear. My snub-nosed .38 wasn't visible, but I could seize it if need be. "Why didn't you tell me about the cache of drugs a week ago?" I rubbed at the sides of my mouth.

Bobby tented his fingers together. Arc light from a passing car flashed across the living room, lighting up the new lines in Bobby's face. It was completely different. Except for the eyes, no-one would recognize him.

"You work divorce cases," he said.

"Yes, I work divorce cases." I shifted, my body no longer cold, my face and eyes tingling with heat. "Divorce. You hired me for one such divorce case." A case that was closed from the evidence I had on Airedale and Nancy. The Ramada Inn. Room 401.

"I know, I know. You got the evidence." He looked away. "But it was all so dirty."

Jesus Christ. What did he want? Pictures of them playing canasta? I sat up, my legs stiffening, The gun close by.

He reached into the lapels of his chocolate-brown suit. The shirt was off-white. He left five hundred dollar bills on the side of the coffee table. The case was dead for him. He was dead. The new face he wore meant a new beginning. "There you go." He pointed at the bills.

Car lights, brighter this time, arced through the living room once more. The whole bottom-half of his face was new, the cheekbones heavier, the chin shorter.

Bobby had a fourth face.

"Bobby—"

"I'm no longer Bobby." He was now Jean Paul Gendron. Advertising man. He had a social identification card, fake birth certificate, everything.

Advertising. What did he know about advertising?

His favorite show was *Bewitched* so he figured what the hell, he could be a graphic designer, a guy with the catch-phrases working on Front Street. "I always was a quick study."

First Oslo, Sweden and now this, Darrin Stephens.

I had to admit, Bobby call me Jean Paul cracked me up. He had chutzpah.

Look, he said, the new face gave him a chance to start over, to find himself, the better part of himself.

"The Road to Damascus, huh?"

"I thought you were Jewish?"

"No harm in keeping up with other people's stories."

He tapped his short chin three times and agreed.

I wasn't so sure about his becoming a better person. Do-overs happen on the playground: hopscotch, tag, hide and seek. I kept thinking about that damn story with the scorpion and the frog and all of us being true to our natures.

"At least I want to try." He stood, hands in pockets. "I didn't like who I used to be—" That person, Bobby now call me Jean Paul, should have died with a plastic bag over his head instead of Nancy, he said, and smiled.

And then I got to thinking of that son of a bitch Cassel walking the earth as Terrien. I was pretty damn sure that he wasn't trying to become a better person.

"Thanks for everything—"

He patted my shoulder.

I wondered what they'd done with his fingerprints. Acid?

He pushed himself up from the leather chair, stretched heavy arms over his head. "Would you have used that gun on me?" He pointed at the pillow.

I guess he had frisked me and searched the room before I awoke.

"If I had to, yeah."

How was I supposed to know which Bobby I was getting? What if he'd held back some Red 45 for himself?

"I figured as much." He frowned, his mouth clicking with disappointment. "Maybe you need a new face, Fuller."

"A fourth face? No thanks." I was happy dealing with the three that gave me hell.

He moved in shadows and crossed over to and through the front door, his shoulders, legs, and the back of his head, briefly glinting through triangles of dark.

I waited.

There was no helicopter.

. . .

Stana couldn't believe it when I told her about Bobby call me Jean Paul's visit.

"Why didn't you wake me?"

I shrugged. I guess I didn't want him to be part of any story, to be interviewed for a story. He was so forlorn, resigned and yet hopeful, and I wanted to preserve his dignity.

Stana huffed under the striped towel covering her face. She was drying the ends of her wet hair, readying for work. She set the clasp on her watch and pushed a bracelet in place on her other wrist. "What's your plan now?"

"I don't know. I'm making this shit up as I go." I wanted Guillame, the ringleader, and maybe they, N'oublie jamais, were willing to throw him over for 811 packets of Red 45. I counted the batch. Twice.

Stana handed me the Ma Bell records she had got from Sal's office. She'd been holding onto them, waiting for me to feel better. "Call the Montreal numbers. Maybe you'll hit the mother lode."

There were several calls made from Adora to five Montreal area-code numbers.

She sat across from me, notepad on lap, hair still dripping from the shower.

I dialed. Breathed in and blurted, "I got the stuff."

The first person paused and tossed a series of French expletives my way. I assured her it wasn't a pickup line. More F-bombs.

The fourth person to answer was the one.

His voice paused, breath catching, like that quiet interval before the referee drops the puck for a faceoff. "What stuff?"

There was something vaguely familiar about the voice. Manly but a kind of whisper as if the speaker's vocal chords had been burned by acid. I wondered if it were Denys

Goyette, the man in the lambskin hat. Something about the timbre of the voice is what I expected to hear in the tones of a hit man.

"Red 45. 811 packets. That stuff."

Another pause, and his voice steady, a regular metronome. "You have it?"

"I have it, pally."

"What do you want for it?"

"Guillame. The chemist—"

"I'm afraid that's not possible."

"I hear you lost the formula. I've got what's left of the 'noble' experiment. Irony intentional, pally."

"No can do."

The way he said it, the accent, the emphasis on the first word, was all wrong. "Come again?"

"I'm Guillame."

I smiled over the phone to Stana. It was a nasty smile, and she looked at her pumps but sat forward nevertheless so that she could hear anything else the pieces of torn tissue paper had to say.

"I guess your little Guy Fawkes Day isn't going quite according to Hoyle, huh?"

"I don't play poker, Mr. Fuller."

"How did you know who I was?"

"We have our operatives. All over Toronto. We know you're in contact with your supplier of Red 45, Bobby Ehle."

"Is Gillian one of your prime operatives?"

He said nothing.

"Can't recapture the original formula, huh?"

"No." Another pause. This one longer, his breath catching. "What do you want for those packets? You can't possibly expect me to give myself up. $100,000?"

"Sure." I winked at Stana. "In tens and twenties. And I want the girl. Gillian, your Toronto agent and prime manufacturer of your wonderful product."

I was just trying to keep the conversation rolling. Gillian wasn't my ultimate target. Guillame was, but I had to get in a room with him to bring him in. It was fun to pretend that I would ever take that kind of payoff.

Think of all the jazz records I could own. Art Blakey, baby.

"Gillian. That's my asking price." Everyone should play the bad guy every once in a while.

"Gillian. That might—be arranged."

"You arrange it, pally."

Funny how quickly card-carrying terrorist creeps give up their own.

"I won't meet you in Montreal. We meet on my turf," I challenged.

"Who said we were going to meet?"

"We don't meet, we don't deal."

Another catch to his breath. Toronto is six and a half hours, he said, somewhere on Wellesley between the Riverdale Zoo and Parliament. "I'll give you the address once we arrive. I'll expect you to arrive in twenty-five minutes of my phone call. It should only take that long from your home on Houston Crescent to the Don Valley and the Bloor-Danforth exit. If it takes longer. The deal's off."

I was surprised with how well he knew my city and where I lived. "I'll wait for your call."

"Do, pally."

That just cracked me.

Six and a half hours to kill. Maybe I'd finally get around to reading *The Girl Hunters*.

"Oh, can we throw in a bonus?"

"You ask too much, Mr. Fuller."

"I am a covetous son of a bitch, huh?" Always pressing, that's how I played hockey, on the forecheck, backcheck, banging my opponent into the boards. "I want the film, the one that shows Cassel killing Nancy Drouin."

"I know nothing about Nancy Drouin—"

"Bullshit. Gillian's into that shit. She gets off on watching people die. She threw me and my best friend at each other, shot full of Red 45, hoping to see us tear away at each other's faces."

"She really got to you, didn't she—"

"We're not talking about me. We're talking about you and your cause. You want the stuff. I want $100,000, the girl, and the film."

He couldn't do that. Cassel's cover would be blown. The world would know he's walking the planet as Terrien, and that the "new" face is the face of a murderer.

I smiled, my third face's lopsided leer, at Stana. She wrote down what she heard.

"I understand—"

"See you later this afternoon, Mr. Fuller."

"Yours in drugs," I said and hung up.

I still didn't have a plan.

But Stana had a story. She wrote feverishly. "I got to get this to the *Telegram*."

I nodded.

Once the story was in, she wanted to go with me to Wellesley Street, but I said it was too dangerous. What about that extra gun, the .45 in your glove box, I could use that, she pleaded. I could be your partner. No.

"Call Sal. Make sure you've got backup. Don't go in there alone."

I promised I would. She kissed my forehead and gathered her stuff, the handbag that looked like a milk crate, and some loose papers from atop the desk in the living room. She rushed from the room, fluttering her fingers behind the back of her head.

I dialed my therapist. "This is Hayden." "Hayden, yes?" I pinched my eyes. My lips trembled, and the room dropped from cool to colder. I wanted to discuss my father, my past, things I hadn't told anyone but Stana. "Hayden—?" I exhaled sharply, the phone a heavy gun in my hand. Stana. I didn't know how I felt or if it were appropriate to feel the way I did, still did, about her. The phone hurt my ear. I could feel my heart in my shoulders. "Hayden—?"

Was it okay to love her. Again. Was it okay?

My inner monolog remained a secret.

I hung up.

And paced and paced and paced.

Twenty minutes later, I called Sal. He picked up on the second ring. "Jesus Christ. My nuts are still sore from where you kicked me."

"I thought you can't remember a thing—"

"My nuts remember."

I gave him the whole setup, the deal I'd brokered with Guillame. Sal promised backup, at least three unmarked cars all along that stretch of Wellesley, right now. Once I got the location, call and they'd move in closer. And then he patched me through to the RCMP and Anne Chevalier.

I got put on hold.

It took a while.

In fucking credible.

Anne Chevalier's voice was breathy as if she had just run eight city blocks to reach the phone. I gave her the setup. I had the cylinders. I wasn't taking them to the meeting, but if she could come get them after I close out this deal, they were hers. I was real close to bringing in the head terrorist.

"You've got 48 hours."

I thanked her for her confidence in me. And, I don't know, maybe because I wasn't sure if I ought to be having any feelings for Stana again, I wondered if maybe Anne would like to go out with me for coffee sometime.

"Sure," she said, her voice full of bleach, making everything bright.

"Maybe lunch too?" I admired her energy, her courage, and I liked her looks: curvy, full-figured, a little plump. I like that. A lot.

I didn't say that part out loud. At least I don't think I did, but my head was sore.

"Hayden—" There was an awkward pause. "I'm not on the same team."

She liked girls. Usually when men asked her out, she'd go on an obligatory date or two, and then let the connections drift away, but with me she felt she could be totally honest, dropping her cover.

"You seeing someone?"

She was. A girlfriend of two years. It was all very quiet. The RCMP frowned upon—

"I understand."

"I knew you would."

"Before you said you weren't sure you could trust me."

"I was wrong."

That made me smile and the back of my eyes hurt with tears.

She promised to stay with this detail and back me up on Wellesley Street. She really, really liked me, she said.

"Thanks."

When I hung up, the smell of Stana's Chanel No. 5 and Parliament cigarettes lingered.

I shrugged my shoulders, fought back more tears, I was a fucking mess from that Red 45 shit, and put on some Hank Mobley, *Roll Call*. I hummed along to "The More I See You."

From my duffel bag, I pulled out one of the cylinders and removed three packets of Red 45. I placed two packets in the pockets of my blue blazer, and one in the corner of my wallet.

From the refrigerator I grabbed a Coke. No ice.

I couldn't sit down, or read, my head and fingers were jittery, stuttering with thoughts, emotions, love, anger, betrayal. Maybe I'd wash dishes. I gathered up yesterday's cups and plates.

The manila envelope with Stana's nude photos was no longer atop my office desk. It wasn't in the drawers either.

She had taken it.

13

I should have figured they'd go off script.

There was no phone call.

Around 5:15 they arrived at my house in Toronto's north end. Guillame wore a gray hat and heavy overcoat, tied tightly, much too tightly for a hot warm afternoon in July. Denys Goyette, who introduced himself with a big flutter of manicured fingers and the terse pronouncement, "I'm the guy who deep-sixed that nosy cop," sported striped pants, a size too small that highlighted his thick thighs, and a fluffy shirt with Edwardian cuffs and collar. He wore white shoes, heavy curved Carmen Ghias for the feet. He smelled of cologne. On his right wrist was a Rolex so that meant he was a lefty. His black lambskin hat was pushed so far back on his head as if to be in another province, maybe even Newfoundland. The fleur-de-lis on his face was crying.

He smiled. There were shadows between some of his teeth.

He wasn't collecting for the newspaper.

Between them was Stana, hands, lower part of her legs, roped. A small tea towel was crushed into her mouth and duct taped in place. The tape was wound three times around her head and hair. It was going to hurt like hell to remove. Her right eye was a pulpy, swollen peach. Denys had acknowledged with a insincere abject nod that he had done much of the preliminary work on her. So much for not working with his hands.

"Can we come in?" Guillame was all politeness, doffing his fedora to reveal a head full of iron filings. The hair was a phony, a low-budget wig cast off from the Harpo Marx collection. The curls just had too much polyester bend to them. Guillame's eyes were dark, chocolate brown. His nose generous.

I thought he had it fixed in Denmark.

Denys pushed the long barrel of his Smith and Wesson against my chest and I backed into the breezeway, then living room, tripping up over the edge of a welcome mat and some discarded shoes. In Denys's other hand was a tripod. Over his left shoulder a bulging tan bag.

"Planning on shooting more home movies? The right profile? It's my better side."

He motioned with the gun, forcing my arms high, and then removed my snub-nosed .38, cracked open the chamber, and let the shells fall, dancing across the coffee table. I didn't like the heavy rain that accompanied their steps. He dropped my empty gun to the floor. A hollow thud, sand in a heavy envelope.

"I got screens, reflectors, in my bedroom closet. Help you bounce the light. Infrared? We can do infrared—"

"Just keep talking smart-ass. You're running out of minute." He smiled and pointed me toward the living room couch. I sat. His accent was French, but the way he dropped the "s" in "minutes" struck me as a masquerade of sorts, like he was giving the Anglo Jew-boy the kind of a Frenchman we outsiders expected to see.

But he didn't know about that young kid who played baseball on the Humber River and cared about social justice.

They shoved Stana into the leather chair next to me, she

toppled chest first and tried to right herself. It was hard to do with her feet and arms tied. She flipped about like she were at Sea World.

The rope was white. Nylon. Slick. Easy to slip out of.

Stana shifted some more, rolled in place with her hip, and slouched low in the chair, her one good eye on me.

One side of her blouse was torn, a shoulder strap to her bra visible. I shot her a quick reassuring nod, telling her I had a plan.

Right. The only plan I had was to pay some overdue Hydro bills. Plan.

Guillame plunked a heavy metal box on the living room's low-riding coffee table. The lid snapped open as if it were a bigger version of an attaché case. Inside the box were four glasses, polished brightly. He placed them on the table, neatly. And then he hauled out a huge beaker that looked like a desk lamp of frosted glass. On top of the beaker was some kind of cap, a white plastic gizmo with a camel's hump. Atop the hump were slits, three lines. Under the slits were carbon-silver filaments, reminding me of the inside of a light bulb.

"Filtration." He smiled. Apparently Gillian Williams got her water fetish from this cat. "This filter takes out impurities. You pour the water through the filter and it drips down slowly in the beaker. Like slow drip coffee, only better for you."

"Uh-huh." I kind of liked coffee, water not so much.

"Uh-huh, uh-huh." His voice, a shadowy whisper mocked me. "Don't play the tough, cool cat with me, shamus. I'm here to break you." He smiled again and motioned Denys away to fill the contraption with water.

"And don't try to rush me." He smiled, the teeth small, tight, perfect. "We've got two operatives outside, watching. Anything happens they've got their orders." One of the operatives had a rocket launcher, or bazooka, or some damn thing. The other an old-fashioned Tommy, Al Capone style.

Sure enough the blocky shadow of a T-bird was visible through the shroud of the living room curtains.

Guillame held up one of the drinking glasses to the light, twirled it about, and approved of its spotless clarity. His hands were rather small.

"The glasses look new."

"They are. Every time I drink, I like using, when convenient, a new glass."

I started to wonder if this cat was a close friend of Howard Hughes.

Guillame removed a small piece of paper from inside his coat, the belt hanging like a limp beaver's tail. I don't know how he wasn't sweating. "9:46 a.m. Stana Younger leaves the residence of Hayden Fuller." He wagged a finger between us. "4:35 p.m., we abduct Miss Younger from the offices of the *Toronto Telegram*."

Water rushed in the kitchen.

"You didn't have to hit her," I said.

"Oh, but we did. She's feisty." He gave Stana a patronizing tap on her bare shoulder. "I like feisty."

There were a lot of things I didn't like, and Guillame was at the top of my 1050 CHUM chart.

Denys returned with the filtered pitcher. It perspired on the sides. Guillame poured a drink. Drank. Denys did the same.

I declined the invitation to join them.

"I'll have a Coke when you leave."

"Droll, Mr. Fuller. Very droll."

"Yeah, droll," Denys said, teeth full of shadows.

"Surprised we knew your every move? We've got operatives watching your house, watching you—" He pointed through the breezeway to the front door. "We even know that the girl's been here for three days." Another finger wag. This time he threw in a clicking sound of disapproval from the back of his mouth.

"Hydration is the center of good health," Denys said, the French accent coming and going. He laughed through his nose and drank some more.

"Needless to say—" Guillame held up a crooked finger for emphasis. "You can't have Gillian."

"I figured on that when you brought Stana—"

"And the story she was going to print?" He reached inside his tight overcoat and pulled out a longer piece of paper, this one smudged with typewriter ink and spits of blood. He read a choice paragraph or two from her column, and then crumpled the paper and tossed it beyond the far end of the couch, where it rested, a fallen planet, on some Dexter Gordon sessions recorded in Paris.

I smiled over at Stana, my lopsided lupine look.

She bravely smiled back.

"No $100,000, Mr. Fuller."

"No $100,000," Denys echoed, his laughter hollow thunder, eyes a dark sky.

"No girl."

"No girl."

"We got here first."

"We got here first." Denys's thunder was now an erratic drum fill.

Guillame drank more water. "Where are the cylinders?" His eyes darkened.

"I give them to you, will you let the girl go?"

"Her. Yes. You. I have other plans for." The bemused glow to his face forced his lips to press against one another.

It wasn't pretty.

I think Denys might have broken a stick because his laughter now was like playing the drums with one hand.

"You ought to bottle that and sell it to the networks. I think they can find a place to use you on their laugh tracks."

Denys pushed down his hat, over his forehead, his face filling with downturned angry wrinkles. He was no longer laughing.

It was somewhat an improvement.

"Where are the cylinders?" Guillame's voice was a set of dull knives.

"I hid them in the basement." I rifled through my wallet, making like I was looking for a secret combination. "In a safe in the basement." I kept looking, through cards, while palming, from under my birth certificate, a red packet that had been peeking out of a wallet's corner like a treasured, unused condom. "No, no. I'm wrong. I didn't put it in the safe." I didn't even own a safe. My hands were now on my hips and I slid the red packet in a pocket. I smiled, tearing an edge of the packet with finger and thumb. "That Red 45 you people gave me sure fucked up my memory—"

"It will do that." Guillame smiled patiently, awaiting my answer.

So damn polite.

"They're in the bedroom closet. Inside a duffel bag." I snapped my fingers, making like my faulty memory was clearing up. I told you I spoke a fluent Brando, a regular actor I was. "That's where—duffel bag." More finger snaps. "Wow," I mumbled. *Wild One* Brando.

My left hand worked the packet, opening the lip wider.

Denys left the room in a rush. He had a low center of gravity, his shoulders moving left, right, as he hustled.

Guillame unzipped the camera bag, pulled out an 8 mm Bell and Howell, placed it on a wooden chair, his back to me. He raised an arm, wagged a finger. "Don't try anything. Remember. My boys outside."

He was arrogant, over-confident. He ought not to have

taken his eyes off me, ever, but the camera, filming, was an obsession with him, his narcotic.

I'm sure he saw himself as the next Alfred Hitchcock.

He wasn't even Ed Wood on a good day.

With his attention focused on just the damn tripod, Guillame adjusted the legs, unscrewing each, trying to get the three to match up. While he tightened the first leg, I quickly lifted the lid off his elaborate Kool-Aid container and sprinkled enough dust in there to kill a corn field.

A second leg tightened in place.

I had already returned the lid.

The third leg was just where it needed to be. Guillame turned back toward me.

Denys sauntered into the room, three cylinders clutched to his chest.

His pants hurt my eyes. Those stripes belonged on a barber shop pole.

"Got 'em?" Guillame wasn't really looking at anything but his tripod.

"Got 'em."

"Attach the camera—"

Denys nodded.

Guillame set aside the small remains of one glass of water and grabbed a clean glass, doing the same bit, holding the glass up to the light, searching for spots, twirling it, before pouring himself a fresh drink. The liquid was clear, the dusty drugs dissolved. Within seconds half the glass was gone.

He topped off Denys's glass.

Denys too drank half a glass.

Good for him.

"I see you looking oddly at me, Hayden. You've seen this all before, haven't you? The unfinished glasses?"

I had. Adora Borealis. The Northern Lights of Beauty.

"I believe your moniker for that visit was Hawley Walker—"

Shit.

Guillame quickly stepped toward me, stopped, knees touching mine, a smile curving his lips into a twisted snake, and then the trench coat slipped off his shoulders.

Her shoulders.

Naked. Beautiful. Small breasts with pert, pointed nipples. An outy belly button, and a golden hump of blond brush over her privates. "You like what you see?"

It was a bit of a freak show to tell you the truth. That wonderful body with Harpo Marx's hair.

"I am Gillian."

Another fourth face. Bobby Ehle became Jean Paul Gendron, re-born, Saul call me Jean Paul. Anne Chevalier was the mousy Leila. Lenny "The Machete" Cassel was now Brian "Spinner" Terrien. And Gillian Williams lived the life of identity confusion, switching behind the mask of her alter-ego, Guillame Clausen.

Or was Gilliam Williams the fourth face for Guillame Clausen? Who was the alter-ego? Bruce Wayne or Batman? My money was on Mr. Mxyzptlk.

"Fourth face?"

I was talking out loud again. I should have figured on the connection between Guillame and Gillian. Guillame is William in French. Dr. Gillian *Williams*. Dr. Gillian, Guillame. Jesus Christ. Criminals, when they pick aliases for themselves, often don't stray too far from their origins. A Julie Benton becomes a Jennifer Boudreau. That's what I learned in my criminology classes at York University, the ones I needed to get my P.I. license. Shit. I guess I should have attended more classes. I got a B in the course. Gillian Willams. Guillame Clausen.

It was as clear as the prosthetic nose on his face, her

face. "That's a phony, too." I pointed.

She removed it. "A little theatrics." She shrugged. She figured if I saw her real nose I'd spot her, dead away. "I enjoy playing, play acting—" She dropped the nose, a mix of putty and wax to the floor. It rested up against my gun.

"Here's the deal." She moved, spinning around briefly like a runway model, her body free of wrinkles, her ass, dimple free.

She was too perfect. Her skin taut, tight, stretched smooth, as if her very body were sealed up in Tupperware.

She'd had a lot of work done over the years, that's why her face was so immobile. "You're going to make love to me." She hadn't liked how I had tossed aside her passes. Repeatedly.

"Make love," Denys gleamed, the one-handed drum break returning. He drank the rest of the glass. Poured another.

Drink up, friend.

He sure had pretty fingers. All manicured and all.

"If I like your performance, you live. If you don't give me an orgasm—" She shrugged.

"You die," Denys smiled, as if he knew of my troubles in the bedroom.

B+ with Stana.

And the topper. Gillian was going to film the whole thing. "That's how I get off." She said this so directly, unashamed. Orgasm or not, she enjoyed re-living the experience, again and again. Later.

"I figured that."

"Take off your clothes." The words were a shadowy whisper, as if Gillian were re-adopting the Guillame voice, the one I heard on the phone, from whimsy to whispers, the two faces of Guillame/Gillian.

Denys pointed his gun at me. "Clothes."

I undressed, taking my time, hoping the Red 45 would soon seize hold of their logic and break them down, animals with less intelligence, giving me the space in their impending irrational chaos to act.

My pants and their heavy buckle thudded against the hardwood floor. Pain rushed behind my eyes and the tops of my shoulders.

You already know the nose was a prosthesis. The hair too is fake, a wig, Gillian said, the female voice returning.

There was a charm-school undercurrent to the voice, no doubt practiced for hours in front of the Wicked Witch's mirror.

Her polite charm was as real as her brown eyes: colored contacts. She didn't remove them. Gillian was always a woman. She had passed as a man for years, covering up her breasts with rolls of Ace bandages. How else could she be taken seriously as the leader of a political revolution?

"This isn't about revolution," I said. "That's just a smoke screen. Revolutionaries don't carry around their own beakers of filtered water, for chrissakes." She and her pals liked comfortable things, bourgeois things. "You're a goddamn poser. What's the Red 45 really for? To blackmail the city of Montreal? At what price?"

"You're a smart man, Mr. Fuller." The male voice resurfaced, filling in the spaces of the female with a heavier thump. "Quit stalling. Take off your clothes."

My briefs stuck to my thighs like a pair of wet swimming trunks. But I finally rolled them away from my skin.

I was naked.

"Not bad," she said, one of her eyebrows raising. "I can see that you are, indeed, Jewish."

"Yeah. And I really like rugulech." I smiled. "Manischewitz wine, not so much."

"You don't seem all that excited to see me."

My skin was covered in goose bumps, but the rest of me, limp.

"Remember, I have to come before you. If I don't, if I don't come—" Her nipples were hard.

I tried to think of Stana, naked beneath me, moving together, moaning, she now on top, me underneath, but those substitution strategies were getting me nowhere, all I could feel was my pounding heart and the seismic shakes of my legs. Sweat coated my upper lip like a layer of fast drying paint.

And there was nothing happening down there, at all.

"Maybe this will help."

She doffed her wig in Stana's lap.

Gillian's bald head, beautifully shaped, round, was contoured with no awkward bumps or ridges. She had suffered scarlet fever as a child and lost her hair. It never grew back. She smiled awkwardly to fight back the tears crowding her eyes. "Hair's important," she said. "Especially for girls. It defines our femininity. It—" Shortly after the illness she started thinking of herself in a new way, taking on a new identity, passing for male. "That's where the power is."

Unfortunately, I couldn't disagree with her.

This might be the permissive society, but it was still pretty much a man's world.

"How about this? Will this help?" She placed my hand on her breast, and guided it there, her wrist over mine. As she was touching herself with my hand, she talked about the past, placing herself here and there. Cassel, Gillian said, knew. Right away. He saw through the mask, knew Guillame was a woman, but he wanted her as a man. "And I wanted him." So she went to Copenhagen for sex reassignment, but ultimately couldn't go through with it. As much as she loved Cassel, she wanted to love him as a woman, not as a man. But he liked boys. To spite him she got a nose job. "It made me girly."

"Uh-huh. I suppose he still likes boys?"

"He still does."

Boys. Fourteen, thirteen.

"He saw me as a boy. He wanted me as a *boy*. That's why I couldn't go through with the surgery." Her eyes brimmed. "How I did love him—"

Christ. What Cassel was now doing in the name of Terrien sickened me. He was probably on a sexual tourism jag, picking up kids in Singapore.

My hand cramped up under the pressure of her grip, but she kept guiding me, toying with the edges of her breast's nipple.

I felt like a family practitioner, not a lover.

I wondered if I should check her tonsils.

"It was all very confusing, Mr. Fuller." When she returned from Copenhagen, she was two people. Gillian, the Toronto plastic surgeon, and Guillame, the French Canadian chemist. "A quarter of a million dollars is our asking price for Red 45—"

She dropped my hand.

"I knew it," I mumbled. "Posers."

"We're business men, people."

"Right. Giving Canada the business—"

"Today, I embody both aspects of who I am. A woman and a man."

"Who she is," Denys said, Ed McMahon to her Johnny Carson.

Her voice slid easily between genders, high low, canaries in cages and torn shadowy whispers. She laughed. "Well, shall we roll film?" The voice, male, again.

I shrugged. I just wasn't into this.

Gillian now sat next to me. Her perfume smelled of a sandy beach, and thoughts of water dripping from a faucet like pulled taffy filled my mind as she toyed with me, down there, along the shaft, around the head, under the head. Her hands were cold.

"There we go, starting to get a little jump—"

"Little jump," Denys echoed.

The film in the camera snick-snicked, catching now and then, before continuing its ticking purr.

Stana closed her eyes.

Gillian slapped Stana's knees. "You have to watch. You don't—get to leave the room—"

Stana opened her eyes. We were across from each her. My lips loosening as I was getting hard in Gillian's hand.

My body was letting me down, doing, in my heart what I didn't want it to do. I felt like a bowl of soggy cereal. "Wait, wait." I had to stall, anything to stop this. I pushed myself to the other end of the couch.

"This isn't time for pillow talk."

"Who was Gray Davies? What's the real story there?"

"Come back here."

I slid toward her, her hand, cold, returned, pushing against and around the head. "Maybe we need lubricant?"

Denys tossed her some.

What was he, a walking drug store?

She squirted a glob in her hand. "Davies, huh?"

"You lived with him two years—lovers?"

"Yes." What she was warming in her hand was, indeed, Jouissance. It worked on men too. Brazilian resins, extracts, aphrodisiacs. "It'll do wonders." "Great," I mumbled, my Marlon Brando lingo resurfacing. Davies, her lab assistant, saw Guillame adjusting his wig one day, and knew that the man was a woman passing as a man. "Don't ask me how he knew, but he knew." She shrugged, a hand full of lubricant warming me.

I was responding.

Christ.

"In two years he was my double—when I needed to be both Guillame and Gillian. He would take on one of those identities. Family outing and a meeting with my fellow scientists—get it?"

"Uh-huh."

"Denys now fills that role. When I'm Gillian in Toronto, he can pass for Guillame in Montreal—"

"The phone call—"

"At George's. Yes." She smiled. "I apologize for the dramatic subterfuge, but I needed to be in two places at once. You were getting too close. Denys was Guillame—" Her smile was full of funeral ashes.

"So why'd you kill Davies?"

She drank more water, pressing her lips with satisfaction. "It doesn't really matter, does it?" Another shrug. "Suffice it to say he tired of his role and wanted—"

"More?"

"More."

"Like you and a quarter of a million dollars?"

"Something like that." Another smile of black crepe.

So she killed Davies, overdose of, "well, it doesn't really matter, does it?"

Keep talking.

In his dying moments Gray Davies's mouth frothed. It took nine and a half minutes to let go.

She captured it all on Super 8. In color.

The first death she filmed.

The car accident was later rigged to hide the real evidence.

I looked over at Denys. "This little story doesn't bode so well for you, does it, Mr. Doubles?"

"Shut up."

"What happened to the French accent, pally?"

Gillian laughed. Denys was originally from Kirkland Lake, Ontario. His father was a coal miner. Denys attended McGill because he had great grades in high school. "He's an honorary Frenchman."

"Bunch of phonies—"

The lubricant had me there more or less ready.

"She'll tire of you just as she did of Davies." I snapped my fingers in Denys's direction. "And then one morning, you'll be brushing your teeth and your mouth will froth over because of some compound she put in the toothpaste. Your days are numbered, pally."

He glanced at Gillian, eyes filling with burning leaves.

"Don't listen to him—" she said.

"You better listen to me," I said. And then I told of a prior conversation, one at George's, and how Gillian confessed that she didn't like Denys.

"I was acting," she said.

"Uh-huh. Acting. You'll get rid of him when you tire of him. Toothpaste. That's my bet—poison toothpaste—"

"Shut up," he said, but the smoldering amber of his eyes was still burning. *I had him. It was the Airedale/Williams setup all over again. Deep down, these two also hated each other. I was counting on that. The oxytocin receptors and anger and hate mixing with Red 45, a killer cocktail.*

"Let's get with the program—" Gillian's eyes colored with impatience.

God, I hoped my people wouldn't be watching over me soon with a lighted shiva candle.

"I'm not doing it. I—I—" *I couldn't allow this, not again, not like before, years of it, three years of it, my father pushing my face into pillows that smelled of beer and sweat.*

"Your mind says one thing, Hayden, but your—" She touched the tip of me. "The little head. It says something else. Let it do your talking."

"No—"

Stana's one good eye was imploring me to go through with it. *Save myself. Whatever it took Just survive, goddamn it, survive. No shame, no judgment. Survive.*

Like I had done before. Like I will always do. Like Dr. Cohen did in Dachau.

Denys's long-barreled gun was aimed at my forehead.

Stana's eyes and face were telling me "do it, do it." Buy more time. Just a little more. It's okay. I care about you. Do it. No judgment, no judgment.

"Okay, okay." I huffed, lungs once again full of flames.

Gillian lay back, a couch pillow propped behind her head, the twisting smile telling me now.

The camera snick-snicked, skates gliding across center ice, but something about Denys's face was wobbly and needed straightening. He quickly reached for what was left of his water, drank it, hands shaking jackhammers. The glass fell to the floor, a bowling ball exploding through pins. The gun followed, slapping the coffee table as the last pin of his control toppled. I got up quickly and kicked his gun away. It skipped and slid under the couch.

"Feeling a little funny, Mr. Kirkland Lake?"

I leaned into the punch and he staggered back to the bookshelf, knocking about a floor lamp. Three books shook loose, hitting him on the head. One was Bernard Malamud's *The Magic Barrel*. Something about that title seemed appropriate.

He clambered to his feet, grunting like Karloff's monster, knocking over the tri-pod, arms swaying in front of him, heavy axes, his attention, hate, on Gillian.

"How long does it take for Red 45 to kick in, doc? I poured a whole packet of that magic dust into your little old Kool-Aid kit."

She pushed up from the couch, glanced at her watch.

Suddenly she looked very small in my living room. Her shoulders were rounding in on her, her face pulling down the last of her twisted smile.

"That's right, doc. You're the one running out of minute."

Her lips parted, but she was unable to speak.

"You know what it does, don't you, doc? You've filmed it before. Filmed Cassel killing Nancy, only you gave Cassel a small dose, I gave you a whole packet. Look at Denys. Will he tear off your face? Or will you tear off his? Look at him. That's you in a matter of seconds." I smiled. "I know you dislike me, but you *hate* him, being *indebted* to him, the Davies pattern all over again—"

"I hate you, you, and—" She shouted French expletives that quickly slid into a groan of inarticulate babblings, as words suddenly failed her. All of her rational brilliance and scientific know-how had slipped into the primordial ooze.

Her arms now swayed like Denys's.

Before she jumped me, he jumped Gillian.

I grabbed Stana, yanked free her ropes, the slick nylon sliding loose easily.

Denys punched at and tore off one of Gillian's eyebrows. Blood washed over the smooth porcelain of her face.

Harrowing animal mewling, jungle cats let loose in my house, filled the room. Thousands of jungle cats, padding, hissing, clawing.

I pulled Stana from the leather chair and we stumbled, barking our shins on the coffee table. I grabbed my .38, my pants, and we hurried to the kitchen. On the way I stepped over a top of an ear tossed to the floor. And a chewed-off finger.

I didn't know whose ear it was. The finger was Denys. I recognized the manicure.

They snarled and grappled behind us. Chunks of furniture yawped and cracked. More glass shattered. Screams escalated.

I undid the heavy tape wound round Stana's head and mouth. It hurt.

She told me make no mind, no apologies necessary. Instead she was kissing me repeatedly.

I found extra shells for my .38 in a kitchen drawer. Loaded it.

With much difficulty.

I slid into my pants. I couldn't get the belt buckled. My hands were shaking.

Stana reached behind me and buckled the belt.

We parted the curtains over the kitchen sink. There were two shadows in a car in front of the Cerlon house. The windows of the house were open. Aldo and his wife Sharon wouldn't be home for another forty-five minutes. The shadows in the car had Tommys. I didn't see a bazooka or rocket launcher.

I called Sal. My voice a rush, high and breathless. I told him to get his fucking motherfucking ass to my place, fucking pronto. They'd pulled a switch and our lives, mine and Stana's, were in a goddamn sling. Hurry. And watch yourself. Two boys in a '64 Thunderbird, carrying Tommy's.

I wiped the edges of my mouth.

"On my way. Hang in there."

The RCMP was coming too. I hoped Anne Chevalier could write me up a commendation, send it to Soupy Campbell, get me back in the NHL.

Hayden Fuller, Canadian hero.

My mind wanders sometimes.

Anyway, the yelling, beyond our sight lines, were now guttural screams, a million drums rat-a-tat-tatting, pound-pounding, and then a crack of bones like the tearing apart of a Thanksgiving day carcass. And we quickly got the sense that somebody was no longer moving and never would again.

More grunts. Pleasing. More bones breaking, separating, tearing of skin, muscle from bone.

Stana leaned into me, an arm around my shoulder. My right hand gripped the .38.

We sat at the kitchen table, her hand in mine, fingers crocheted together. I hoped that whoever out there had devoured the other was wanting a nap after dining.

Soon I might have to kill whatever thing was still out there.

Then I'd shower and put on some fresh clothes.

But for now we waited, Stana and me, and waited and waited for Sal Lambertino.

About the Author

GRANT TRACEY is an English professor at the University of Northern Iowa, where he teaches film and creative writing, and has been the fiction editor of the *North American Review* for over seventeen years. He has published nearly fifty short stories, four collections of fiction, and articles on Samuel Fuller and James Cagney. His collections are *Final Stanzas, Lovers & Strangers, Parallel Lines and the Hockey Universe*, and *Playing Mac: A Novella in Two Acts, and Other Scenes*. In 2016 he published his debut crime novel, *Cheap Amusements*, the first Hayden Fuller Mystery. Grant is editor of the Gas Station Pulp mystery series published by North American Review Press. Thrice nominated for a Pushcart Prize, Grant was the recipient of an Iowa Regents Award for Faculty Excellence in 2013. In addition to his writing, editing and teaching, Grant has acted in over thirty community theater productions.

Other Twelve Winters Press titles
from master storyteller Grant Tracey

Cheap Amusements
Book Club Edition

Grant Tracey's debut
Hayden Fuller Mystery

"Sexploitation, hidden cameras,
murder . . . a lot of fun."
— Robert Hellenga,
author of *Sixteen Pleasures*

Paperback - Hardcover - Kindle

Final Stanzas
Stories

Eleven spellbinding tales

"With the compelling force of
cinema, these stories pull us into
the deepest recesses of the heart."
— Steven Schwartz,
author of *Little Raw Souls*

Paperback - Kindle - Audio

twelvewinters.com - @twelvewinters

Award-winning fiction titles
from Twelve Winters Press

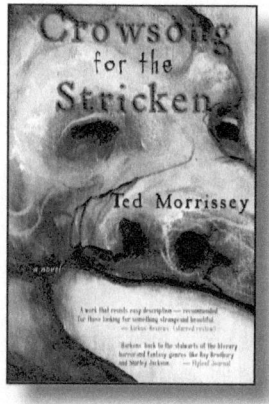

Crowsong for the Stricken
a prismatic novel by Ted Morrissey

Winner of the International Book
Award in Literary Fiction 2018
from Book Fest

A Kirkus Reviews Best Indie Book
of 2017. "Strange and beautiful."
— *Kirkus Reviews,* starred review

Paperback - Hardcover - Kindle

The Dying Athabaskan
a long story by Brady Harrison

Winner of the
Publisher's Long Story Prize

"Lyrical and lush, harrowing and
humorous, daring and dark."
— Prize Announcement

Paperback - Kindle

twelvewinters.com - @twelvewinters

www.ingramcontent.com/pod-product-compliance
Lightning Source LLC
Chambersburg PA
CBHW020105180626
46812CB00006B/2475